HUNTING ARMED MEN

JM ERICKSON

OTHER WORKS BY J. M. ERICKSON

Science Fiction

Heavy Weight of Darkness

Endless Fall of Night

Afterlife Code

Time Is for Dragonflies and Angels

The Prince: Lucifer's Origins

Future Prometheus: The Series

Intelligent Design: Revelations to Apocalypse

Action/Adventure Thrillers

Albatross: Birds of Flight—Book One

Raven: Birds of Flight—Book Two

Eagle: Birds of Flight—Book Three

Falcon: Birds of Flight—Book Four

Flight of the Black Swan

http://www.jmericksonindiewriter.com

Editors: *Kirkus Editorial*

Cover design: Cathy Helms, *Avalon Graphics*

www.avalongraphics.org

Publisher: Emergency Comms Press (ECP)

https://www.jmericksonindiewriter.com/

https://www.jmericksonindiewriter.net/

https://www.jmeindieblog.com/

https://www.instagram.com/jmerickson_writes/

ISBN (D2D ePub Format): 978-1- 942708-62-9

ISBN (D2D Soft Cover): 978-1- 942708-63-6

WARNING: This work does contain material, themes, and situations involving slavery, graphic language, the sex trafficking of young men and women, and racial slurs. This book is for adult readers.

He who fights with monsters might take care lest he thereby become a monster. And if you gaze for long into an abyss, the abyss gazes also into you.

—Friedrich Nietzsche, *Beyond Good and Evil: Prelude to a Philosophy of the Future,* 1886

PROLOGUE

CASSIE FELT great pressure growing in her chest with every passing second. The sensation of being strangled was palpable, and her limbs weighed as heavy as lead bars. Even though she was immobilized and mute, she heard herself screaming, "No, no, no!"

Suddenly, she felt firm hands on her, moving her. Not in a violent, threatening way, but almost a controlled fashion, as if trying to wake someone.

"Cassie? Cassie—it's all right. I'm here. You're safe," a woman said.

Cassie felt herself sit upright, gulp in air, and place both hands to her bare chest to find the source of the pressure crushing her. There was none. Just skin.

Her body was wet from sweat, and it took her seconds to reorient.

"It's all right, Cassie. You're good," the woman said again, her voice reassuring and soft.

Cassie looked around and saw Penny had pulled her out of her nightmare. She was one of ten roommates who shared living spaces in many crevices and caves embedded in the midrange mountains surrounding two of the more active volcanoes.

Cassie tried to center herself first with her breathing and then with moving her limbs, as if to make sure she was truly awake. She was. She felt much better. She looked out of the small cave's opening and saw the grand view of the mountain range, and how the improved light in the cavern seemingly enhanced the lava flow below. She then looked over to the cave interior and saw an array of mostly made bedding, with personal effects and clothing, clearly reminiscent of a college dorm, an image she had long since forgotten.

That was a lifetime ago, she thought.

"Did I wake anyone? I'm sorry," Cassie said.

"No, hon. Everyone has gone to eat, and we wanted to let you sleep. I came up to check on you, and you were having another nightmare," Penny said.

Cassie nodded and started to move out of bed. She was naked, as was the custom in the Martian underworld with its persistent heat and humid air. Lately, ever since she'd destroyed the garrison on the surface miles away, there had been an improvement in airflow, and the interior cavern was significantly less dark, bringing the light index up to a perpetual twilight or early dawn.

"You going to be all right, Cassie?" Penny asked.

Cassie nodded she would be, and stretched her back, rolling her shoulders and feeling herself recover.

"I'm fine, Penny. Thank you for waking me up. Sorry if I disturbed you," Cassie said.

"Don't apologize," Penny said as she stood up to leave. "Do you want something to eat? Robert cooked up his famous blend of meat with flavored water."

"Yes, please. I'll be down in a few minutes. Save a plate and a spot," Cassie said.

"You got it, hon," Penny said.

As soon as she was gone, Cassie moved to her water basin. It was filled with cave-temperature water, a holdover from the night before, now available to splash her face.

Cassie was drying her face when she wondered where Alethia, her implanted AI, was.

"I hate when you have nightmares. I can feel you having them, but there's nothing I can do to wake you," Alethia said.

Slowly, an image of her AI emerged on her optic nerve displaying a young Black woman dressed in Martian garb, with multiple knives tactically placed on her outer carry rig and a recent addition, a sidearm hanging off her hip. This martial appearance ran in stark contrast to her deep brown eyes that conveyed warmth and kindness and a smile that radiated peace and calm.

"I really wish you could too," Cassie said.

A moment of silence passed. As was their custom and comfort, there was never a rush to fill the void. Theirs was a strong relationship that didn't need chatter or idle conversation. Cassie had come to appreciate silence, not needing to keep the conversation going.

"Ever since Bennett told you he had gone to the Delta Exchange, and he had, most likely, seen all the stuff you did, the nightmares have gotten worse," Alethia said.

"They sure have. As soon as he said he had seen *the horror* I saw, I knew it was true. How else could such a patrician asshole man do a complete change of heart unless he had firsthand seen the truth?" Cassie said.

"Were the nightmares about the Delta Exchange, or those disks you saw? The ones documenting the genocide around the globe?" Alethia asked.

"The genocide. The firsthand survivor interviews and then their subsequent executions. This time the prisoners looked like they were of Southeast Asian descent, and some others looked Middle Eastern. It was just horrible. Their blank expressions, speaking clinically of what happened—the fireball and toxin, carnage and troops pouring in . . ." Cassie felt her breathing getting shallow and her heart racing.

"Just breathe, Cassie. You're here with me on Mars," Alethia said, her voice level, calm, and firm.

"Normally, I would say, 'You're safe,' but that would be a stretch, seeing we're on a hostile planet, danger all around and above, and you're reaching to still greater heights in the realm of military genius or terrorism, depending on whom you ask. I mean, just saying, we are by far both the most dangerous and most wanted outlaws in the solar system," Alethia said.

By now, Cassie had stopped drying her face and had refocused her attention back to Alethia's image, which had taken a relaxed stance, leaning up against an invisible wall while inspecting her fingernails.

"So, this is supposed to help me feel better," Cassie said.

Alethia stood up straight, moved her hands to her hips, and looked back at her.

"Nope. Just grounding you. And speaking of grounding, and not to be that nagging friend, but you really shouldn't carry the burden of leadership alone," Alethia said.

Ugh. Not this again, she thought.

"I have you and my, ah, girlfriends here," Cassie started, gesturing to the empty beds.

"You know no one is here, right? And the beds are empty," Alethia said.

"You know what I mean. I have close relationships with my friends, Gavin, Nancy, the doctor, and a lot of people," Cassie said. "And it's not like I've got nothing to do. That oasis you located and we found—that's a big deal that's keeping me busy."

By now, Cassie was collecting and putting on her clothes, as scant as they were, and affixing her gear, which were exclusively edged weapons, her blowpipe, and her rifle.

"I'm not denying any of that. I'm just saying, sooner or later, you're going to want to put all of this to rest, and grab the happiness you are entitled to. You've done more than your share to expose the lies on Earth, and you have pushed off any plans Earth might have had about crushing Mars's independence. Between Earth's internal strife and limited resources, and your crushing their offensive strength, I think you are allowed to call it a day, find someone to be happy with, and as soon as we confirm the oasis is real, you, well, actually, we should go," Alethia said.

There were times like these when having such a personal, implanted AI persistently in your head—who knew every detail about you, and whose design was based on a clinical psychologist—was difficult. The truth about a situation was always exposed, and escaping into a lie was impossible.

Cassie stopped to collect her thoughts. She thought about a possible argument to counter Alethia's point, but that would be a waste of time. Alethia was right.

"I hate you," Cassie said as she started her descent to join the others.

Alethia smiled, and her image began to fade.

"Call me if you need me," she said before popping out of existence.

"You bet," Cassie said.

As she descended into the cave, there was an uptick in moving hot air, most likely because of the torches lighting the way and the layout of the caves that allowed for cross drafts, providing a much-welcomed breeze. As she moved deeper, she could hear voices of men and women engaging in conversations with periodic bursts of laughter and excitement. The aroma of cooked meat completely dominated the interior, overcoming the constant smell of sulfur, phosphate, salt, and ozone.

Cassie felt a small smile form on her face as the opening revealed well over thirty people of all genders, shapes, sizes, colors, and abilities, all engaging in different groups, having their conversations and eating. Something she could never have imagined when she was back on Earth, and could never fathom she might play a role in establishing on Mars.

Who the fuck knew this could happen? she thought.

"Cassie! Cassie, come over here! Janet and Dave were telling us this rumor that there are giant underground squids around some of the former ports," Penny yelled out.

This drew a roar of laughter at the absurdity of such a thing.

"Really? We got three-headed dogs the size of a second-story building and cats the size of a shuttle craft, and you think an underground squid couldn't possibly exist? Are you high on mushrooms again?" Janet countered.

An even louder laugh erupted.

Cassie waved to them and headed in their direction to sit, eat, and talk.

Alethia, as always, was right. She was entitled to enjoy these moments, these times of connection and fellowship. It did help her feel less lonely.

1

MARS—2158

THREE YEARS LATER . . .

—...

FIRST OFFICER ROBERT LEE VI, executive officer of Earth interplanetary spaceship the *Robert E. Lee*, reviewed his most recent, encrypted communique from naval intelligence and his updated orders from the admiralty from a secured station far from his office and from the sight of crew members. Escaping prying eyes was far easier these days since a quarter of the crew had abandoned their posts to live on Mars, and the captain did nothing to keep it from happening. This laissez-faire management style drove him crazy. But then, his boss, Captain T. J. Jackson Taylor, was well known for breaking rules, following his own path regardless of privilege, protocols, and orders. The captain had gone native—switching out official naval uniforms for field BDU from Fort Deadly and rogue colonial outposts, trading energy batteries and some raw material for disgusting Martian "food" and near-extinct firearms that used gunpowder. Taylor even allowed the crew to mingle and work with non-Patrician classes as if they were equal, even adopting some of their grooming habits—all of it was vile. Just the thought of eating the meat that came from the surface, interfacing with the plebian or surf, wearing the "updated" battle dress uniforms, all made him want to throw up.

"No strength. No commitment; no honor," he muttered to himself. He adjusted his ship uniform neckline and pulled his sleeves to his wrists, the way they were supposed to be.

"No focus or purpose," he said.

These were all frequent statements he constantly made under his breath that had escalated to nearly every hour of every day as the weeks, months, and years ticked on. It had been only weeks since real, palpable hope was on the horizon.

He had been waiting for this moment for a long time, and finally, it had arrived. After months of encrypted reports of Captain Taylor's trading Freeport, not being aggressive in finding the hijacked *Raleigh*, and still no efforts to retake that deserter Bennett and kill the rebel traitor Cassandra Kurtz, the orders had finally come in after close to three years. They were short and to the point, and about time.

> Earth Admiralty and Tribunal Command confirm recent orders for Captain Taylor of the Robert E. Lee to initiate aggressive steps to find and secure the Raleigh, refit it for return to service, regroup with the task force in search of Cassandra Kurtz, and support defending the colonies. If he does not comply with these orders within seven solar days of receipt of this dispatch, you are authorized to take command of the Lee and carry out his duties. You will have latitude as to who will need to be detained should there be resistance. Success of this mission and key points will result in field promotion to captain and significant increase in pay and benefits.

XO Lee noted that the time stamp was three solar days ago, leaving the captain four days left to comply with the admiralty's orders. If not, he could seize command, and his birthright to the *Robert E. Lee* would be attained, finally. He couldn't help but smile. He had acknowledged receipt of his orders with zeal and had since then struggled with the charade of keeping his emotions in check, especially when giving sitreps and attending status meetings. Still, it soothed him every time he had to hold his tongue when he saw the "captain's crew" wearing those new BDU around the ship, or plebs and surfs being in restricted areas for Patricians only, or even hearing the crew in the mess hall actually favoring the "new" food from the surface. It was all disgusting otherwise.

Before these recent orders, he had been thinking about returning to Earth and calling it a career. He couldn't stomach dealing with such a passive captain and his weak-ass command team.

"Two fucking years, and we got nothing—no Kurtz, no slaves, no obedience from those outposts, and no control," he said aloud.

Adding insult to injury, the medication that kept his genes in check and slowed aging ran out a year ago. Since then, he'd experienced hair loss, and what was left was converting back to lighter brown hair. The weight gain, decreased bone density, and reduced muscle mass all required increased exercise, duration, and rigor, all necessary now that a monthly injection no longer kept everything at bay. The benefits of Earth's artificial general intelligence in medicine decades ago now had been lost due to distance, lack of resolve from the captain, and failure of duty. He was angry to watch his body slip into decay, becoming more plebian with every passing week. It was easy to see that many of his crewmates were feeling the same way. The ones that wore their ship uniforms with pride—no updates, augmentation, or Martian influence—saluted him with respect.

I believe in honor, duty, and my earned status. Every loyal naval officer does, he thought.

All except for the captain, and his close-knit command team: the doctor, the chief engineer, and the security chief. They aged seemingly without regret or remorse, almost reveling in the challenge of returning to a premedication state, as if fighting to regain some youth from exercise, physical excursions, and fasting were somehow a game to them.

He reread the document, almost to ensure he was not imagining it. After another read, he folded it, put it in his uniform's inside pocket, stood, adjusted his cap over this thinning brown hair, and left the sequestered room with a firm gait, chest out and chin high.

Things are about to change around here, he thought.

He felt the corners of his mouth lift. It had been a very long time since he'd felt a smile on his face.

As soon as he arrived at the midship, a nexus leading to five corridors to different sections of the ship, he was surprised to see the security guard, Lieutenant Henson, a close friend and ally, and no friend to Captain Taylor and crew, loitering at the hub, as if waiting for someone. As always, he was dutifully wearing his ship uniform, as were the two crew members standing behind him, a cook and a security guard who looked serious in contrast to Henson, who gave his best friendly smile and positive voice.

Lee slowed his pace, surprised and curious as to what was happening. For a moment, he was worried that his three compatriots would turn him into the captain. Of the remaining crew, there were only eighteen like-minded, faithful soldiers of the admiralty left on the ship.

"Good afternoon, XO. I got those supplies you were

asking for," Henson said while pointing to the bags just out of sight behind the other men.

Lee could tell his friend was posing, acting as if all was well, while underneath, the gravitas of what was to follow was easy for him to feel and see.

"We have a short window, and a shuttle from Mars Sector 108 has just landed and is prepping for immediate dust-off," he continued.

As Henson spoke, he guided his hand to the XO's shoulder and redirected him with a firm, nonaggressive grip toward the shuttle bay with the other two men in pursuit.

"Shit," was all Lee said.

The entire interaction told a story he had hoped not to get at this point—retaking the ship was blown, and he and the others were about to be arrested as both conspirators to seize his ship and loyalists to the admiralty.

"When?" Lee asked.

Moving at a quick pace, Henson continued smiling, providing immediate intelligence as he navigated the sparsely populated halls to their escape ship.

"Ten minutes ago. I heard Grisson and the captain talking about an encrypted inbound message one of the analysts deciphered. They were heading to armory with the chief en route and three of my junior security guards. Since I was not included, I figured they know who most of us are, and that it makes sense to escape while we can," Henson explained.

Lee nodded at all the key points. He was happy that Henson had been on his side from the beginning. He had planned on installing him as his own XO once he'd dealt with the present traitorous command crew. Now, he had to move to plan B.

"What's the play, *Captain*?" Henson asked.

The sudden change in rank was not lost on Lee. No

longer part of the existing command structure under Taylor and his idiotic crew, he was a true patriot of Earth's admiralty. The title *Captain* now meant they were outed, and their own self-contained unit.

For command with all its privileges, duties, and honor.

Suppressing a smile and not missing a beat, Lee outlined their next steps.

"We regroup on the flight deck, seize a shuttle, engage Freeport to secure intel on Kurtz, track her, find her, and kill her. Bring her head back to the admiralty, and we'll all be rich, reinstated with the full rights and privileges of our birthright, including my ship," he said.

Clear. Concise. Steps of a clear leader, he thought.

"She always should have been your ship. Taylor defiled your legacy," Henson said.

*Perfect word—*defiled *is what he did. Taylor is the true traitor here!*

"You are damn right, *XO* Henson. We're about to make that all right. We should have this all done in a week, two weeks before our admiralty ships arrive from Earth."

He could tell that Henson was smiling at his own field promotion.

"All we'll need is a deck of cards," Henson said.

Just ahead, Lee saw five other members of his new command structure, all waiting just outside the portal to the flight deck. All nodded, acknowledging a new page was turning. These men had multiple laser rifles slung confirming they had either just raided or collected an array of weapons over time for this very moment. As they dispensed each laser rifle, energy packs, and various edged weapons, each man conferred with the other, some meeting for the first time as their communications had been sealed off into cells for security reasons.

"Food? Water," another man asked.

Lyman, the cook, answered. His voice was surprisingly deeper than his small stature would imply.

"Two-week field rations and water behind ventilation panel eight."

There was a sudden drop in activities as the men looked at the cook, obviously upset at the limited supplies.

"Comms? Radio gear?" another man asked.

"Roberts was on his way from engine room's tech ops, but I got nothing more," Lyman said.

More frowned expressions emerged. Only Lee and Henson were not concerned.

"Our first stop is Freeport to secure more supplies and a base of operations. We are soldiers, men. Officers of Earth's admiralty. I think we can handle half-dressed, brown savages whose most advanced weapons are rifles and knives. Pull your shit together," Lee said.

"Snap to attention, men! *Captain* Lee is speaking."

Without a misstep, each soldier stood erect and faced forward without expression.

A long moment passed before Henson spoke again.

"Sorry about that lapse in discipline, sir. I thought we had true believers."

Lee nodded in agreement. He was about to continue with more inspiring words as they waited for the rest of his new crew to arrive, but the internal klaxon erupted into life, and an all too familiar voice boomed over the internship comms.

"This is *your* captain, speaking. All hands: Find and secure Robert Lee, former XO of *our* good *ship*, by any means necessary. Any and all conspirators aligned with him will be caught and punished. This is not a drill. All hands—capture and secure Robert Lee and all his compatriots for arrest," Captain Taylor announced.

"It's not your ship," Lee muttered to himself.

Just as the announcement stopped, Lee turned in the

direction of running feet. Rifle now trained downrange, Lee kept his team from shooting as soon as they heard and saw laser discharges hitting the wall first, and then more laser beams shooting back. Lee turned to Henson, who confirmed his thoughts—whoever was heading in their direction most likely were his men, under fire by the captain's men. Sure enough, three men running at a frenetic pace were shooting back as they hurtled toward Lee and his crew. Without hesitation, Henson shouted out orders to the others as Lee waved his insurgents on.

"Eben! Conroy! Breach the hatch! Rhett and Truman, secure the ship and set up a perimeter. Find Glenn—get the shuttle prepped for immediate launch with minimal safety distance. The rest, get the supplies, and kill anyone who resists," he said.

Without hesitation and newfound motivation that they were all going to be caught, court-marshaled or worse, the men sprang into action. Lee watched in pride as his men broke through to the flight deck and carried out their orders while he and the others locked down the only entrance, the blown hatch, with covering fire, pushing back anyone who attempted to advance. Seconds seemed like several minutes as they held their positions while their supplies and escape route were ready for dust-off.

Henson came up beside Lee and the others with a young plebian man, a mechanic by the look of him, who was wide-eyed, frightened, and clutched a small courier bag.

"Captain—you and the others fall back now! I'm sending this plebe to give a package to the captain," Henson said.

Lee looked at his newly appointed XO, back at the scared boy and package, and back again to Henson. Lee smiled and nodded approvingly.

Desperate circumstances, desperate measures. At least the plebe's life will have meaning now, he thought.

"All right! Everyone—fall back! Regroup on the shuttle, and prep for emergency launch," Lee said.

As he and his men retreated, Henson picked up the covering fire and then shouted back to the encroaching attackers. After the last volley, with half the distance to the shuttle covered, Lee heard Henson yelling something back but couldn't make out what was being said. He slowed his forward motion and turned to see what was happening. He was surprised to see Henson racing toward him while the young man holding the package stood in the breached hatch, hands up, obviously responding to the approaching men as he started to fall to his knees with his hands behind his head.

"Go, go, go!" Henson yelled, racing toward him in a dead run.

Lee ran to the shuttle door where Lyman was standing holding a small black device in his hand. Lee looked at the cook, who seemed surprisingly calm and yet focused on what was happening behind Henson at the doorway. The plebe was still on his knees, facing an unseen force. Henson was now within feet of the shuttle when he gave the order—"Send it."

Lee looked directly at Lyman, who without hesitation flipped the trigger guard and pushed the detonator.

The explosion's flash came first, brilliant and blinding if you didn't avert your eyes fast enough. Then came the deafening sound followed immediately by the energy blast. If it wasn't for the fact that Lee was holding on to the hatch's handrail, he was positive he would have been on the flight deck in pain.

With Lyman and Henson now jumping into the shuttle, Lee made sure he was the last man to board the escaping ship, all choreographed to ensure he was still perceived as a true leader. As the shuttle door closed, he could hear the blast area's release of internal pressure and loss of air, now escaping into space. The ship slipped toward the blast site and the gaping hole he presumed was left not only in the ship's interior but also imagined in Mars's orbit.

"I'm sorry I damaged your ship. I had to make sure those slackers would be busy so we could exit and land without incident," Henson said.

Lee nodded with approval, even though he felt bad that his namesake had been damaged to ensure their escape.

"Desperate circumstances, XO. Desperate measures," Lee said.

"I'm sure the *Lee*'s refit will be spectacular when we get back to Earth," Henson said.

"It will," Lee answered.

The shuttle jolted forward and thrusters fired, making getting to their seats difficult. All his men were in their seats, leaving the front two open for him and Henson. As he took his seat, balancing from falling into it, he thought he saw another person, maybe a woman, in the back, holding her head as the shuttle bolted forward.

After he buckled himself in, he was about to ask who was sitting in the back row when there was a muffled explosion, pushing the ship hard to port, and electrical arcs erupted from the lights. No dimming; just popping. The shuttle's intercom came on. The pilot spoke.

"The *Lee* hit one of our starboard engines. Half the shuttle is on batteries, and we're about to enter the atmosphere. Expect some chop," the pilot said.

"If it were Earth, we'd be screwed, but it's going to be a rough landing," Henson added.

Lee pushed the intercom button on his command chair.

"Can we make Freeport?"

The response was slower than he had hoped, but it eventually came.

"We should, but we're in for some turbulence, and it might be a harder landing than hoped," the pilot said.

"Okay. Make it happen," Lee said.

Lee nodded and gave Henson an affirming look.

"We are sailing into history," he said to the XO.

The shuttle began to shudder, then was buffeted by a growing mix of Martian and earthlike atmosphere from the planet's terraforming factories.

A golden age for a growing empire, Lee thought.

2

"NOW, THAT'S NICE," Willard Bennet said.

Bennett could already feel a smile on his face, even though he thought he was still asleep. He might have been, but he was stirring now, feeling some aches return to his left side and back from yesterday's work. Far from heavy lifting, ploughing, or pulling, he assisted the young cadets in gun maintenance and bore sighting, then some shooting drills, reminding them of how to use cover and when to attack versus retreat. While there was little in the way of military action, Lt. Commander David Strong of Fort Deadly was a stickler for weapons readiness and emergency drills. Fortunately, Virgil Johnson, former bridge officer of the *Lee,* now a field officer of Lefties Rangers—a name both a tribute to Bennett and an inside joke—did all the real training that mattered in the Mars underworld. Tracking, finding, and capturing rogue mutant creatures running riot in the wild reduced their threat and provided much-needed medical and protein sustenance. Johnson also helped train anyone who wanted in the arts of war—close-quarter fighting, field combat, special operations, active defense, and siege. The military training was an evolving curriculum. Earth's naval and terrestrial military operations and standards were ineffective in a hot, humid environment of perpetual twilight, forever enveloped in light Martian dust, sudden gusts of hot wind, and a pungent, almost mold-like smell of sulfur and methane, all against the backdrop of a constant red glow from lava riverbeds and volcanoes. There were areas of shifting sands, now inhabited by other genetically altered, still-not-identified creatures, and landscapes of boulders and mushroomlike fungi the size of large bushes and small trees. Mars was truly alien to Earth, and none of the day-to-day activities they could do back home could easily be done, if at all, on Mars. Anything high-tech in the field was near useless. The persistent static electrical discharges sapped energy rifles' battery supplies. Firearms using gunpowder, glass binoculars, old-style radio wave comms—all the old tech was state of the art on Mars, and all the new and improved Earth tech was now raw material for important things like edged weapons, clothing, utensils, or trinkets.

From a scientific perspective, what really took Bennett and everyone else by surprise was the constant volcanic activity on a planet where plate tectonics, seismic activity, and magnetic poles were not supposed to exist. But then, the introduction of nanobot technology and massive atmosphere converters on a planetary schedule probably altered the smaller planet's science. Alien technology added to a non-Earth world for years was probably bound to make unexpected changes, much like when the colonists wanted docile white dogs and cats but accidently created monstrous creatures destined to break free and terrorize the foreigners.

Hubris, Bennett had often thought.

But right now, he swore he felt as if he were on a tropical island with warm sand and a light warm breeze, bathed in sunlight, overlooking a deep, dark ocean of water, untainted by debris, floating cities of garbage, and fuel slicks. It was an image he had been dreaming of more often, not from personal experience but from memories of pictures and books he had discovered while on his Martian exile. The images and books found not on Earth but on Mars were the source of many enjoyable dreams in the last three years. Of all the things he had grown to love about Mars, this was an unexpected joy that continued to pay dividends.

"Are you awake, sir? Commander Strong was hoping you could join him for coffee," a young male voice said.

Bennett shook himself to wake up faster. While he would have preferred to sleep longer, his military training wouldn't allow it. He still had agency and was not going to let old age keep him base-bound, let alone in bed. Still, he did enjoy sleeping later, and the occasional nap. While being close to sixty on Earth was nothing due to medical advances, here on Mars, all those advances were gone, leaving raw physical work, fasting, sleep, friends, and a purpose to keep a person fit, strong, and alive.

So, this is what getting old is like. Not too bad, he thought.

Bennett opened his left eye, sighed, and moved from his left side to his back, allowing his biological limbs to get their feeling back. Initially, looking straight up, he then turned his working eye to his right side and saw a young, biracial youth, maybe eleven years old, holding Bennett's cane, a towel on his shoulder, and an extended hand to assist him with getting out of bed.

In his earlier years on Mars, he would never have accepted such support. Over time, he began to understand the wisdom he'd first heard about accepting help. Specialist Betsy Ann Hall had told him that to adjust to his new body, he would need to accept help from others. The timing of that advice, after losing his right eye and right hand as keys to weapons of mass destruction, was not lost on him at the time and had stuck with him since.

"Did I oversleep again, Knowles?" Bennett asked.

"No, sir. I woke you before first shift. Commander Strong saw me heading to your barracks and asked if I would get you going sooner. Scuttlebutt is that something is going to happen or already has on the *Lee,* and Captain Taylor wants us and Freeport to be in the loop in case unwelcomed visitors arrive planet-side," Knowles explained.

Bennett sat up, swung his legs over but waved off Knowles's hand to assist. Knowles stepped back, recognizing that Bennett wanted to see if he could stand up from the bunk without support as a means of testing his strength and balance. Bennett felt his feet on the warm, carved Martian ground of the barracks, and without using his hand or hook, he stood. As his ritual was to wear his "sleeping" BDUs, a light gray material that wicked moisture away from his body, there was no need to search for clothes to start the dressing process. Sleeping in one's battle dress uniform was the norm for everyone at Fort Deadly. The difference with Bennett was he was not active per se, and he was allowed to wear more Martian-made clothing. It was times like this, not needing to get dressed, for example, that allowed him more time to focus on important things, not to be dragged down with more morning preps.

"Success," he said.

Just as he finished the word, he could see that his vision was beginning to gray, and he became suddenly lightheaded. He felt two hands brace him up at the torso, and he let himself be helped.

"Dizzy, sir," Knowles said.

"Yep. Strength is good. Blood pressure is high. You know, Knowles, it sucks getting old," Bennett said.

He was surprised he wasn't bitter about it as a former captain and a Patrician; he had had full access to health- and life-extending medication, biannual injections and supplements to keep him fit and younger with little exercise and effort needed. After years without this medical intervention—the space travel prior to his arrival on Mars, his post-Earth incarceration and subsequent release—his body was reflecting its age, wear, and tear. Still, if he been less active, less involved in his new Martian home, he would have died years ago. Movement, activity, friends, and purpose kept him in the game. A game he never thought he would be in: Instead of retiring in opulence, health, and privilege, he was working, focused on a Martian frontier with coworkers who were his friends.

Bennett shook his head to refocus his thoughts. He looked down at his feet, legs, hand, and hook and could see he remained lean and strong, but he probably should be eating more protein. Then he remembered Knowles talking about the base captain wanting to meet him for coffee. Something about intelligence on the *Lee* orbiting Mars.

"Hey, Knowles, how do you know what's happening on the *Lee*? When did you get military clearance? Are you part of Strong's intelligence team, or are you running your own deep-cover spec ops on Taylor's ship?" Bennett said.

The youth laughed. Knowles was clearly a preteen but had a maturity that was pervasive with younger people in the Martian frontier. He was happy to see that all the young people, which included nearly everyone on the base, had a sense of humor and optimism. It was contagious.

"No, sir," Knowles said. "I was clearing plates from the comm center, and the guys were talking about encrypted messages that were intercepted. Commander Strong was conveying a brief sitrep to the watch commander. Sounds like there will be some action soon. I'm not sure what, exactly."

"Okay, Knowles. Keep me in the loop," Bennett said.

After two more steps, Bennett's head felt completely clear, and he no longer needed Knowles's support. He took his cane and moved out to the hall to exit the barracks. It was quiet with little movement. Without the need for light to see, not that there was any more light than dark shadows, Bennett headed to the latrine. With Knowles on his left side, he could see the lad remained a step ahead with a towel still hung on his left shoulder, a satchel hanging off his right shoulder, and a larger-than-average canteen that Bennett deducted was his washing water.

He handed Knowles his cane, entered the latrine, and began the morning with a good bowel movement and a steady stream of urine. He was pleased for several reasons, but mostly because these bodily functions were key indicators that his digestive system was still working well. On Mars, those basic functions were key indicators of viability. If they were off, sleep problems came into play, and then fatigue, immobility, and death was soon to come. The base medic was a stickler for everyone to be aware and to let him or the commander know if there was a problem.

Enjoy the little things, he thought. Yet another pearl of advice he had heard all his life but had only truly believed after arriving on Mars.

Happy to conclude his business, Bennett exited the latrine and moved to a waiting basin of water to wash, shave, and rinse. He was in the middle of applying shaving wax sparingly to his face, a precious resource to anyone wanting to be clean-shaven, when he heard Knowles ask the question most of his cadet aides asked most of the time.

"So, sir, did everything come out okay? How are you feeling?" Knowles asked.

Bennett smirked. As far as presentation, Knowles was better than most in asking such a sensitive question of an older adult. He liked Knowles, so he answered the question with a question first.

"Now, did Hall recruit all the cadets to do a daily medical check on me, or was it the chief medic's order for you to ask me?" Bennett said.

Knowles did not hesitate to answer.

"Both, sir. Specialist Hall scheduled a rotating team and gave us clear instructions of what to ask and when to ask, and to report our findings to the base medic. Sergeant Burns asked me to be ready to catch you in case your blood pressure was high. He is also worried that you are dehydrated and working too hard, sir."

Bennett nodded in approval of Knowles's explanation.

"You can let them know all my organs are doing well, and I'll do my best to drink more water," Bennett said.

"Thank you, sir," Knowles said. Clearly, the youth was appreciative of accomplishing his mission. Bennett knew full well what it was like to disappoint both Hall and Burns, two people who obviously cared about others and insisted on cooperation to keep everyone safe.

"I understand, Knowles. Those two can be difficult," Bennett said.

Bennett began to shave, a morning routine he was privileged to be able to do with so few luxuries as wax soap and washing water. A small mirror and another cloth from Knowles's satchel made such an activity pleasurable. Adjusting from his dominant right hand to his left had taken a while to adapt, but he found that his shaving technique had improved, and his right hook had a phenomenal grip to the point where he had to be careful not to break the handle of the mirror he was holding. He chuckled at the thought that should he break another mirror, it would add to last month's additional seven years bad luck.

As Bennett positioned the mirror to shave, he did a once-over to see his entire face and head: With his nearly bald, thin face and unexpectedly tight skin, the only real grooming work was to shave any facial stubble and get rid of the minute hair on his head. He thought back to when he'd first shaved everything when he'd first arrived. It had been the best thing ever. The head of hair he'd kept when aboard the *Lee*, or any ship for that matter, was miserable to maintain on

Mars. If the humidity, sweat, and abject heat didn't kill you, the head of hair would make you overheat faster. With the exception of nonmilitary people, mostly young women, having no head and facial hair was the norm, profoundly different from Earth.

"Knowles? Since you're so well connected, do you know when Virgil will be back?"

"Field Officer Johnson? He's an easy sol day out from here, maybe farther. The Third Platoon and Eighth Civilian Militia from Freeport Twelve wanted an advanced course in recon, scouting, and foraging. Word is they are going to be the last ones out covering Freeport's last convoy to the Promised Land," Knowles said.

"Thank you, Knowles," Bennett said.

Bennett smiled to himself at Knowles's polite correction of Virgil Johnson's rank and duties.

Hmm. The Third Platoon was the third group of Freeport colonists that were trained by Lt. Commander Taylor and Virgil. Wow! It's close to three years, Bennett thought.

"Sir," Knowles said, "what is this Promised Land that Freeport and the guys talk about here?"

Bennett nodded at the question while carefully navigating the odd angle of his left hand reaching under his right ear without crushing the mirror.

"A couple of years ago, Kurtz created a task force to head out beyond those peaks and far beyond the lava beds, closer to the equator to see if the topology was different. She, well, her AI had accessed some old charts, reports, and documents originally thought to be destroyed, and they discovered it was true. It's an oasis of sorts, where the methane gas, Martian dust, and plate tectonics are less active. Apparently with the terraforming plants and nanobots, there was a tipping point in the atmosphere and immediate biosphere. I mean, it's not paradise, but it is less hot and humid, no spontaneous electricity bursts and dust everywhere, and there's water and vegetation. It's odd, but that part of the underground is far enough to be different, but it's still one planet. Pretty crazy," Bennett said.

"And this AI? Is it in her head? It has a name?" Knowles asked.

"Yeah . . .that's a longer story," he said.

Bennett started his mental gymnastics of how to explain that Kurtz, once part of the ruling class of Earth's elite, had privileges that he and a small select group had while the majority did not. He struggled with how to explain his own origins, how he was sent to kill her, and for a short time he wanted to until he found out what happened. There were times he wished he never did. Ignorance was bliss. But then, for whatever reason, being with Knowles, telling him about the past, being a part of a frontier community, part of a brave new world order—he was glad to have this all instead.

It took a moment, but Bennett had an idea of what to say. With every passing explanation to the youth and young people he met, he had gotten better at being accurate, clear, and to the point. He was determined to keep the record straight for his own frame of mind, if not for Martian records.

He just finished his last stroke without drawing blood and breaking the mirror and was rinsing his face with the basin wash water when he saw a glimmering light, a bright yellow and orange, emerge high up in the horizon, in the direction of where Fort Sumter once stood. Then a shockingly loud blast front ripped through the massive cavern world.

"What the hell?" Bennett said.

He stood up straight and watched what looked like a shuttle drop suddenly from the highest parts of the cavern, eventually leveling out, spewing light and blue fire as it streaked across the darkness. The front and midsection of the ship vacillated between orange and green, probably partially ignited methane, but a solid blue flame from just one thruster indicated there was a problem. As it passed above, the already heated air was warmed even more, and the blast front wind caught up with the light and sound of the descending shuttle craft.

"Wow! That's crazy! You think it will make it?" Knowles said.

Before Bennett could respond, Fort Deadly's sirens kicked on. Squads of men and women of varying racial backgrounds, all uniformly dressed in their BDUs, moved as one coordinated force, all focused on getting to their posts. It was evident that Lt. Commander Strong's and Virgil Johnson's training and drills were second nature.

"There you are, old man. You'd better be getting a move on and keep up. LT's been waiting, and he doesn't like it when his coffee is cold. And he'll show no pity for the disabled, aged, and infirmed," a voice from behind said.

The voice, low, strong and robust, came from none other than W. T. Sherman, chief engineer from the *Lee* on loan to Fort Deadly to get the underground aqueducts to work. As brutal and unpolished as the engineer could be—an officer Bennett could never have worked with if he had his old ship again—he had come to admire, respect and genuinely enjoy Sherman's company.

Knowles snapped to attention and saluted as Sherman approached.

"Drop the salute. You hear that siren, Knowles? Anyone seeing you salute me would know I'm an officer and could snipe me down. You want that?" Sherman said.

The smirk on Sherman's face, difficult to see in shadows and perpetual dusk, was clearly visible to Bennett.

"One can only hope, Sherman. Maybe next time, Knowles," Bennett said.

Knowles dropped his salute and looked puzzled by

Bennett's response. Sherman looked genuinely pleased at the quick retort.

"You are fast at something, Bennett. You catch that show? Whoever is on that shuttle better hope and pray they have a great pilot. There are only two pilots on the *Lee* that could manage it. Aft thruster is burning hot, and atmosphere methane is partially burning off. I hope they make it," Sherman said.

Bennett was impressed by Sherman's rapid assessment.

"You can tell all that from looking at it, sir?" Knowles said.

"Hmm, some of it. It helped that Lieutenant Davis flashed me a digital message that the XO made his move, damaged the ship, and the captain ordered a shot to disable than destroy," Sherman said as he displayed a small, screened device that clearly displayed a message.

"You do have skills," Bennett said.

"And backups to the backups. I'll see if I can rig up something similar for you and the crew here," Sherman said.

"Obliged," Bennett said.

Sherman was still striding, not slowing down, which meant Bennett and Knowles had to keep up the pace. Sherman, part of the *Lee*'s command structure, was similarly groomed and uniformed like personnel at Fort Deadly, a great departure from the expected white, blue, and red uniform expected on ship and planet-side. Captain Taylor had adjusted his resources, tactics, and strategies for the long game, far more adaptive and useful for a long stay on Mars. Bennett remembered when he'd first arrived in his uniform. He'd eventually shaved his head, dumped the uniform, and roamed the Martian underground in his compressed undergarments like Hall and Virgil.

Wow. That was a while ago, he thought.

"You know what this is all about?" Bennett asked.

"Maybe. The captain has been aware of his XO's

shenanigans and left some breadcrumbs to test the water. I almost didn't come last week because I had a feeling shit was going to go sideways, and I didn't want to miss the action,"

"Never asked to the party, eh, Sherman?" Bennett said.

"It's always been a thing. I find I fit better with traitors, deserters, and insurrectionists; I appreciate their moral compass," Sherman responded.

"Seriously, though—mutineers? Doesn't Earth's admiralty frown upon that?" Bennett said.

"They sure do. But the captain was positive that the XO's anger and resentment would blind him, and he would never doubt the veracity of an order from Earth if it meant getting his own ship, his great-great-great-granddaddy's namesake," Sherman said.

Heir apparent, Bennett thought.

He remembered how fast and thorough the entitlement could reach. How ambition could blind and cloud judgment. He pushed the unpleasant memory away and focused on the next steps. Speaking of next steps, Bennett became aware of his breathing and the quick pace Sherman had set. While not winded, dizzy, or straining, he knew it wouldn't take long for all of those symptoms to arrive if he kept this up. It was evident that Knowles was aware of his situation as he was staying very close behind.

A low, reverberating boom echoed through the cavern. It was hard to tell if the ship had landed hard or just crashed. As there was no plume of blue burning light from a distant crash, Bennett was hopeful.

Still, he was worried. His friend Betsy Ann Hall was out in the wilds again, doing her research and recon for Kurtz, while Virgil was out training in the same general direction. Both were capable, far more than he was and had ever been. Still, he was worried. Less out of responsibility and duty and solely out of fear and anxiety for their well-being. They were his family.

"Don't worry, Bennett. If it's the XO, his sights are only on Kurtz and her people and getting his ship he thinks he's entitled to. He has no personal beef with your people," Sherman said.

As caustic and abrasive Sherman could be, he was frighteningly intuitive, a great read of people, which endeared him to all who knew him, and unflinchingly loyal to those who worked with him.

"You are such a softy, Sherman," Bennett said.

"I am aware," Sherman said.

Ascending two short steps, Sherman was now holding a thin screen door open to the comms center for Bennett and Knowles. With no need to keep small bugs out, the screen door was an anachronistic holdover from Earth's farmlands. Decorative not functional. Bennett liked it.

The hall entrance was short and broke into two rooms. On the left was the communication center, Bennett's immediate objective. There was a young cadet, Olsen, he remembered, who was adjusting the receiving dial.

"Bad copy, Bravo Alpha. I repeat, bad copy, Bravo Alpha," Olsen said.

Upon seeing Bennett and Sherman, the young cadet, close to ten years old, stood up, saluted, and gave up his seat for the senior officer to take over. Without hesitation, Bennett took his seat, grateful to have stopped speed walking. The communication station was a giant throwback to the day's prior transceivers, with dedicated radios for transmitting and receiving rather than combining them. While transceivers worked well on Mars, separate receiver and transmitter radios and specialized antennae made transmission in their undergrown world near crystal clear. While spontaneous static electricity swarms could erupt anywhere and anytime, the dust devils that stayed around the Fort Sumter crater that could interfere with radio waves were short lived.

Suddenly, Betsy Ann Hall's voice came through clearly and strong.

"It looks like a damaged survey shuttle in distress heading to Freeport. No mayday, running silent. Might be her comms are down along with their running lights. She's burning from a plasma burn on her starboard side consistent with laser scaring, not reentry failure. Foxtrot Delta Six," Hall said.

Bennett was relieved to hear his friend's voice. It was strong and curt, reflective of the owner. He took a moment to figure out what to say based on what he knew.

"We're on open comms. I bet they can hear everything we say," Bennett said to Sherman.

"The captain and I locked down all the working comms equipment except for two damaged ones left to take. Even if they did, I doubt someone is monitoring comms as they plummet from the sky—if they make it, it will be rough, and they'll have to depart and get distance. I'd be brief," Sherman said.

"Good copy, Bravo Alpha. Downed shuttle could be mutineers from the *Lee*. They damaged the ship, and the captain retaliated. The XO believes his mission is to capture-kill Kurtz to get his ship and career back. Blind ambition. Very dangerous. I would avoid. Although you are not likely the targets, you and all of us are probable collateral if any engaged. They're going to start at Freeport, I would guess, work their way to the mountains, and pass by you. Return to base or link up with Victor Juliet and elements of the Third Platoon and civilian militia group. Copy, Bravo Alpha," Bennett relayed, referring to Virgil by his initials in the military alphabet.

There was a moment of silence, as if the recipient was either processing or writing down instructions.

"Good copy, Foxtrot Delta Six. Returning to base or link up with Victor Juliet, copy," Hall said.

"Copy, Bravo Alpha. Return to base or Victor Juliet and attached elements," Bennett said.

As much as Bennett didn't want to put Hall and Virgil in danger, he was still a soldier, a member of Fort Deadly and those he felt under his charge. He looked at Knowles and Olsen and thought of all the young men, women, boys, and girls he was responsible for.

Bennett keyed up the transmitter again.

"Bravo Alpha—update: Link up with Victor Juliet, observe, recon, scout, and test strengths. If engage, deadly force authorized. Deter and defend at will. Contain if possible. You are weapons free. Sitrep every twenty from top of the hour starting at 07:00. Shit is going to get real, Bravo Alpha. Watch your six. Foxtrot Delta Six out."

"Good copy, Foxtrot Delta Six. Bravo Alpha out," Hall said.

Bennett noted the time and turned to Olsen and Knowles.

"All right, Cadets, you're on comms duty. Rotate coverage per hours and instruction, and get two other cadets to break up comms and run messages to Lieutenant Commander Strong. No saluting; we're on alert."

"Yes, sir," both youths said.

Bennett stood up to relinquish his seat and post to Olsen, who seized the comms as if at the wheel of an old navy ship.

Bennett moved past Sherman, who clearly yielded to him leading and setting the pace. He was going to brief the commander, whom he suspected was already aware of everything that had transpired.

There was a stillness in the air as the two men headed out the door to the command bunker. The activity had come to a standstill, with everyone at their posts. Bennett could barely see outlines of sniper spotters at elevated points. All light had been doused, leaving twilight illumination for the early

Martian morning. There was a silence between Bennett and Sherman. Bennett was curious why his peer was unusually quiet, but he kept walking.

"Inspiring demonstration of command, sir. It will be yet another example for field command and leadership for the young to talk about for years to come. Oh, the decisiveness and conviction of it all," Sherman said.

"Shut up, Sherman. No one likes you," Bennett said.

3

CASSIE WATCHED Hall from a safe distance. Even though it was early in the morning, with no day or night underground on Mars, it being early or late in the day was moot, but somehow, it mattered. Cassie was tired and lay prone between two vents throwing more heat around her, in addition to the lava river. She remained still, peering through a small monocular, a telescope she'd traded at Freeport for her "great journey." Her subject, Betsy Ann Hall, was a mere one hundred feet away. Clad in her usual black compression top and bottoms, Cassie did her best to move slowly and not let the sweat bother her while she moved at glacial speed. With the sole exception of her knife, she was glad to have left her full armament in a cache as it would have been a major burden to keep quiet and most likely to reveal her location. The heat waves most likely obscured her position, with curly, wavy heat coming from the surface, disrupting any image that was close to the ground, and far enough to talk to Alethia without being overheard. The other benefit of being between hot vents was the absence of humidity. While the change in constantly breathing persistent warm air and the salty aftertaste that permeated the entire Martian underworld atmosphere seemed novel, it didn't last long. The heated air was barely breathable and dried out every orifice and pore while tasteless grit accumulated at the back of her teeth, irritating an already itchy tongue. All of this, when she arrived, was difficult to adjust to, and she never thought for one minute that she would, like so many Martians, adapt.

Still, it was hot where she was, and she had a mission. A focus.

She could see that Hall was done with the light maintenance on her rifle and was getting herself ready for some kind of rest, an hour of light sleep maybe before she continued her trek. She scanned Hall's immediate area and saw she still had two handheld radios spilled out from her initial cleaning, along with a satchel of food or maybe medical supplies. Hard to say for sure, with the heat waves obscuring her own vision, along with sweat. Cassie was happy she had cut her red hair short again before this mission. She would have been more miserable with the longer hair she had grown. It was a dark auburn that closely matched her skin. With the medication for genetic expression and extension for life long since gone over the years on Mars, she was totally herself physically, and time underground surrounded by heated air probably added to other physiological changes. Everyone on Mars—former slaves, plebes, surfs, original colonists, and former Patricians—all were Martians now. Earth's vestiges of class rank and social order were nearly all gone. Strict class lines, expectations, and racially bound behaviors all interfered with the number one rule for survival on Mars—the ability to rapidly adapt to a constantly changing environment.

Cassie sighed and refocused on her mission.

Based on Alethia's assessment, Hall was heading back to the cave where she and her compatriots had been held captive nearly three years ago.

Cassie put her telescope down, wiped the sweat off her forehead, and spoke.

"She must be returning to the scene of the crime to see if she can find some clues. She's a persistent individual," she said.

"Or she's set on settling the score and plans to track you so she can kill you. I mean, you have no idea what kind of relationship she has with Bennett," Alethia said.

Cassie shook her head in confusion and disbelief.

"Weren't you the one that figured out that Bennett had changed? He really can't return to Earth and is stuck here. Didn't you convince me that he wasn't even interested in killing me, and that he was just done with all the bullshit?" Cassie said.

"Yes, but she's a mix of class, and maybe she hates you over him, one over the other. Conflicted or something. I don't know, but maybe she has an allegiance to Bennett or his bosses and will try to kill you as you sleep one night," Alethia said.

"Maybe, but I doubt it."

There was silence in her head for a moment. She continued watching Hall checking on her perimeter warnings, which were more than usual as she was in the open, close to the lava river and heat vents to keep most of the creatures away—not all, but especially the humans.

"Yeah. When you say it out loud, it sounds like a convoluted conspiracy, psychobabble. I'm just trying to keep us safe," Alethia said.

"I know, and I appreciate it," Cassie said.

A moment passed. Silence.

"So . . .why are we here?" Alethia asked.

Cassie quickly responded. It was scripted and prepared.

"Threat assessment and intelligence gathering."

Cassie took a closer look at Hall's prosthetic left leg below the knee. She watched how she walked around, her short hair length, how she moved her hands, how she transitioned from fine motor control to gross motor, and transitioned back. She was pretty, in a simple, basic way, but Cassie found her spirit, intelligence, and tenacity the most attractive. Her clothing was loose to allow for comfort but still had a uniform look. It was a light color, khaki or beige, maybe. The only thing truly native to Mars were her sandals, clearly made from Freeport that were perfect for the hard, dusty terrain, both cool and comfortable. Cassie had the same kind except hers had thicker soles and laces that traveled just below her own knees for further support and better wear and tear.

"Or we're here for personal reasons, like you're dumbass in love with her, or just lust," Alethia said. Her words were casual, no tone, surprise or teasing. Maybe a hint of annoyance, as if she had been aware of something Cassie thought was well hidden.

Cassie clenched her back jaw and tightened her grip on her spyglass.

"Okay! How would you know that unless you were able to dig into my mind? If we weren't friends and you weren't hardwired into my brain, we'd be having serious discussions about boundaries and removing you to a computer chip," Cassie said.

I knew it! What else has she seen in my head? Cassie thought.

"Really? You think I had to read your mind to figure this out? The doctor called it when he saw you interact with her at the cave. You remember? Years ago. Now, what was it he said . . . 'Your attention seemed divided between the captain and the specialist,'" Alethia said.

Cassie remained quiet. She had to give her that one.

"And then, the first thing out of your mouth to Gavin and Nancy after a two-year recon mission of searching, finding, and coming back with the map to get us all to an oasis on this hot, barren red planet, was your interaction with Specialist Hall—again, pointed out by the doctor," Alethia added.

Yeah. That was stupid obvious, Cassie thought.

"And then last year, we spent an entire month 'observing' how she and that Virgil Johnson were training the new arrivals, ex-slaves, plebes, and surfs from Freeport for a month—a full month—when a week would have sufficed," Alethia continued.

Cassie pursed her lips and felt heat flush her face.

"And six months ago, we just had to determine 'proof of change,' you said, and we carefully watched Hall and Bennett for three weeks work with Freeport's adults and all those children, teaching first aid, vegetation identification, and survival techniques. I mean, five days could have confirmed all of that, but for some reason, it was imperative to closely watch and confirm how they interacted with the locals when we are slated to leave this heated hell."

Cassie dropped her head in embarrassment.

"*Heated hell* is redundant," Cassie muttered. Alethia ignored the weak distraction.

"Really? That's all you've got?" Alethia said.

Cassie felt more evidence building up to a crushing defeat.

"And since you have no interest in men, and you're still human, it's easy to see that you might be lonely. Even if you wanted to be a regular person and drop this Kurtz persona Earth has labeled you with, you would be hard-pressed to find someone you are both attracted to and like-minded . . ."

"Okay, Alethia. You're right. Okay. You win. So, can we get back to work here?" Cassie said.

Alethia stopped talking in her head for a moment. In lieu of that, her image appeared on Cassie's optic nerve. She hadn't changed much except to have shortened hair instead of braids, an assortment of edged weapons, and less clothing like Cassie did, as if she also felt the persistent Martian landscape and, underground heat the way everyone else did.

"You see? The truth will set you free," she finally said.

"Hmm."

"You know my name means *truth,* right?"

"I know, Alethia. It's not the first time you've mentioned it. Now, can we get back to work?" Cassie said.

Cassie continued her surveillance and scanned potential approach vectors.

"The only thing I'm seeing is stalking. And since I really can't read your mind, and we've established you like her at least and are attracted to her, can you tell me the plan? Why are you here, and what do you want to do?" Alethia asked.

Cassie sighed.

"What are your intentions, Colonel Kurtz?" Alethia asked, referencing the main character of a book from where Cassie's name was based.

Cassie put her telescope down, placed her hands under her chin for support, and took time to really figure out what she wanted to do. Alethia, modelled after an early twenty-first-century human psychologist, waited and allowed the process to continue uninterrupted.

Minutes went by as she continued to think. After much mental gymnastics, internal discussions, past and present, intellectual posits and counterarguments, Cassie felt as if she could answer the question. She remained in the same position, though she still scanned her area now and then as Hall seemed to struggle with falling asleep. Whether it was the heat or lack of sleep or just overall fatigue, this was the first time Cassie had ever seen Hall dozing off.

"This is all a guess, but I think Hall and I are similar. She's not a Patrician but not a pleb or surfer either. She's clearly capable of living out here in the wild, but she must have been able to manage the political blood sport on a ship to get here, and clearly earned the admiration of Patrician men, which is next to impossible to do. I think she's capable of fitting in but is out here instead. She communicates back to their fort and others in the field, but it's not a sitrep, more social. I wonder if she's tired of all things, people and Earth, and if she would want to have an adventure with someone who kind of gets her, and not be lonely in being free," Cassie said.

As Cassie spoke, Alethia's image remained still, except for her nodding for her to continue.

"Honestly, I'm lonely, and I'd like to go to our new place with someone whom I could get to know better, and who might be like me," Cassie said.

Alethia was still as if she was thinking and then nodded before she spoke.

"You might be right. And what I am hearing is that you are lonely, and you think she is too, and you would like her to come with you. It really makes sense. I mean, it's a big ask. You're asking her to drop everything to go with you, Earth's greatest terrorist, on a four-month journey, to a new discovery, a not fully reconned and thoroughly explored land," Alethia said.

"You know, when you say it like that, it makes that it sound like I'm out of my mind," Cassie said.

Alethia struck an all-too-familiar pose with corresponding expression; she looked down at her feet that were shoulder-length apart, rocking back and forth while looking at her sandals, with her hands behind her back as if she were truly contemplating as a human might.

Cassie decided to continue with her thoughts before her AI friend provided a balance of pros and cons to her argument, a preferred technique she had noticed over years of cohabitation.

"Not just any land, but a land of conifers; small oceans of fresh water; cooler climates where you need fire to get warm;

corn, unbelievably; and plenty of wildlife for hunting. The actual Promised Land," Cassie said.

"All true, almost too true. Let's hope she believes you," Alethia said.

"So, if she were to leave her radios behind for radio silence, take the four-month trip after everyone has gone, there's no risk of exposing the main group," Cassie added.

"And the sentries along the route will help; yes, it's all good if she comes. And finding such a place on this world, no one in their right mind would want to leave," Alethia said.

The conversation stopped for a moment.

"So, what are you waiting for? You already know she's alone. You've seen her trip wires, and it won't take much for you to disarm her before she even knows you're there," Alethia said.

"I can be silent when I move," Cassie said.

"A shadow. Stealth is your strong suit," Alethia agreed.

There was more silence. Cassie continued to survey the area, marking out her approach, and already knew how she would disarm Hall if needed. But there was a big thing getting in her way. She was thinking about how she would explain this to Hall without sounding juvenile, like an immature teenager.

"Cassie? Are you still with me here?" Alethia said.

"I don't know if she'll even like me," Cassie blurted out.

Alethia's image froze for a moment. Then her jaw slackened, then tightened into a smile.

Ah, come on! Are we really doing this third-grade processing? Cassie thought.

Alethia's smile was small, but to her credit, she did not berate or embarrass Cassie. Instead, she gave her advice that she was sure a non-Patrician therapist would have given more than a hundred years ago.

"Cassie, it makes sense. I'm not going to be an asshole

here. I'm just going to say this—you had an abbreviated childhood, no teen stuff, no young adult stuff like friends, intimate and otherwise. Then, due to your convictions of equality and fair play, you became a terrorist put in prison, then sent to Mars, almost enslaved into marriage, and then you become a leader for all non-Patricians on the planet. No time to have a moment or two for what might pass as a 'normal' private life. So, here's the deal: If you don't ask, you won't know, and she won't know," Alethia said.

Cassie remained still and took her time to process all that Alethia said. It was a lot. It was important.

"Nothing worse than not knowing," Alethia added.

"I suppose the great Cassandra Kurtz really has been too busy to have a social life," Cassie finally said.

"Absolutely. So, tell her exactly what you told me about wanting her to come along. It's genuine, truthful, no bullshit, and she will be impressed with the honesty, and your seeming ease with yourself, your power, and your person," Alethia coached.

"Yeah. I should be able to do this," Cassie said.

She looked through her glass again and saw Hall was awake but not looking in her direction. She got up into a crouch to head left of her position. She stowed her telescope away to free up her hands when she moved.

"Unless she laughs at you and thinks you're entitled egotist to think she would drop everything for you. Kind of ballsy, you know," Alethia added.

Cassie dropped to the ground again as if dodging a sniper round zeroing in on her head. She was back in her prone position with her head buried in her hands.

"Fuck! I'm out. Stupid, stupid, stupid," Cassie blurted out.

"I'm just messing with you, Cassie. You can do this. You've taken on the patriarchy, racists, a self-entitled caste system; freed slaves, surfers, and plebes; and you've shown them a new way to live—free to live where and how you want, love who you want, and to be your genuine self on a new planet. I think you can ask another person to join you on a new quest," Alethia said.

Logically, Cassie knew that Alethia was right, but she still lay face down, not moving.

"Honestly, after what you've been through, don't you think you're entitled to a little happiness?" she said.

Cassie let a little more time pass before she looked up, pulled herself together, pushed adolescent embarrassment aside, and stood up straight, then moved like she had a purpose.

"Okay. We're doing this. So, when she's looking at you, make sure to don't slouch, and keep eye contact as you talk. Don't be afraid to push your boobs out just a little more if you could. I mean, you're not working with much, but . . ." Alethia said.

"Okay, if I'm doing this, I can't have you in my head. It will be too distracting," Cassie said.

"No problem. We'll do an after-action report when she's asleep," Alethia said.

While Alethia's term for gossiping after she asked Hall for a date was a bit more militaristic than social, Cassie let it go.

"To the great journey," Cassie said.

"To the Promised Land," Alethia said.

Cassie moved slowly at first, drifting to the left with the plan to shift right between two small venting holes before she gave a wide berth to circle behind Hall. There was a set of large rocks that could conceal a prone body easily. She was about halfway to her designated spot when she heard a suppressed sonic boom. Cassie immediately dropped flatter into the ground, as if that were possible, and observed Hall was now standing looking in the opposite direction. With Hall's attention focused 180 degrees in the opposite direction, Cassie leaped up and bolted the several meters necessary to get behind her under cover of rocks. Once there, she peeked out to see Hall rummaging through her pack for her binoculars and searching for the source of the noise.

Cassie followed her actions with her own scope right before another boom echoed much louder than before, its sound waves carried by the increased oxygen and cavern walls. Even with the blood-red illuminated background of crimson, white and yellow lava flows, the ceiling above was heavily bathed in shadows and darkness, with only faux buildings the terraforming nanites had duplicated upside down on the cave's roof and walls. With all of this as a background, Cassie made out a familiar shape. It was enveloped in a yellow-orange bubble with a blue flame burning it: a spacecraft, more likely a shuttle, that was clearly damaged.

"Ah, Alethia? Are you seeing this," Cassie asked.

"Seeing what? I got out of your head to give you some space . . . What the hell is that? I'm gone for a minute, and shit is falling from the sky," Alethia said.

A strong wave front pushed more heat in her face as the shuttle arced over Hall's and her position. The only upside was that the pouring sweat was nearly evaporated by the heated, compressed wave. Cassie dropped behind cover as Hall's gaze now followed the craft in her direction and carefully continued her own assessment of what she was seeing: a recon-survey shuttle, unarmed, sometimes used for transport of personnel and small missions. This was the first time she had ever seen one suffering potential catastrophic damage. She had seen enough of them. Some had been looking for her and her tribes; others would be on the frontier, exploring, while most others would trade with Freeport and other colony outposts. And while this one was following a course directly to Freeport, it was unclear if it would have a soft landing.

Before she could say anything, she heard Hall talking far closer than she remembered. Cassie froze against the rock and ground. It sounded like Hall had halved the distance between them. Cassie now hoped that she would not stand on the rocks she was plastered against to get a better view.

"Repeat. Bad copy, Kilo Charlie One," a very young male voice came through.

"Hall is nine feet away to the left of the rock. She has her radio on the highest setting, and it sounds like her gain is to its limit," Alethia said.

"You can hear that?"

"It looks like a damaged survey shuttle in distress heading to Freeport. No mayday, running silent. Might be her comms are down along with their running lights. She's burning from a plasma burn on her starboard side consistent with laser scaring, not reentry failure. Foxtrot Delta Six," Hall said.

"Good copy, Bravo Alpha. Downed shuttle could be mutineers from the *Lee*. They damaged the ship, and the captain retaliated. The XO believes his mission is to capture-kill Kurtz to get his ship and career back. Blind ambition. Very dangerous. I would avoid. Although you are not likely the targets, you and all of us are probable collateral if any engage. They're going to start at Freeport, I would guess, work their way to the mountains, and pass by you. Return to base, or link up with Victor Juliet and elements of the Third Platoon and civilian militia group. Copy, Bravo Alpha," the radio voice said.

Cassie pressed farther into rock and ground, listening intently.

"That voice is our mutual friend, Willard Bennett, former captain of the *Jefferson Davis*, now turncoat of the admiralty and philanthropist of Fort Deadly, Freeport, and all fellow Martians. He's made some serious changes and life choices over the years," Alethia said.

Cassie remembered him immediately. Initially, Cassie had hated Bennett from the very moment she'd met him in prison and more so when she was on his ship. Her plan to take his eye and hand from his dying body to sabotage the orbiting ships at the time and destroy the garrison on the surface would have been the perfect revenge. It should have been an experience of joy and pleasure. Instead, she had witnessed something unexpected from the darkness—he had changed. Not just physically, but he seemed kinder, open to all as equals, begged for his friends' life at the forfeit of his own, and was less than interested in killing her. She actually felt bad in needing to disfigure him to complete all her objectives. Still, after all of that, he was not bitter. He was, based on all her observations, witnesses, and reports, a changed man, focused on helping others. An example of redemption and adaptation.

"Copy, Bravo Alpha. Return to base or Victor Juliet and attached elements."

"Good copy, Foxtrot Delta Six. Return to base, or link up with Victor Juliet and attached elements, copy," Hall said.

There was a moment's delay. It was brief, but it was clear that Foxtrot Delta, or Bennett, was revising the plan to a more assertive approach. The update also sounded as if it was fading.

"Bravo Alpha—update: Link up with Victor Juliet, observe, recon, scout, and test strengths. If engaged, deadly force authorized. Deter and defend at will. Contain if possible. You are weapons free. Sitrep every twenty from top of the hour starting at 07:00. Shit is going to get real, Bravo Alpha. Watch your six. Foxtrot Delta Six out."

"Good copy, Foxtrot Delta Six. Bravo Alpha out," Hall said.

The last acknowledgement sounded farther away, as if she had moved, retreated to where she was camped.

Cassie cautiously looked out to see Hall moving first to

her campsite, then beyond to find and reclaim her perimeter alarms. Once it was clear that she was moving beyond her camp, Cassie ran as fast and as close to the ground as she could to get to Hall's backpack and satchel for key intel—a broadcast frequency to talk and receive on the radios. While she had an urge just to steal one transceiver, she knew that anyone else might forget one in all the excitement of breaking camp and rapid for redeployment, but not Hall. Another person might overlook the missing extra radio, but not her. Cassie scanned each radio's frequency, both offset by 5 hertz in high frequency, 20 megahertz, plus or minus five.

"Got it," Aletha said. "Looks like they found the right frequency for propagation in the cavern's ceiling. It took them long enough."

Cassie had long since dropped the radios back in place and was already on the move making good distance from Hall and her campsite before Alethia chimed in.

"Now, you do still have your transceiver, right? I mean, it would be embarrassing to get all that data from a well-executed intrusion and escape and not have a radio to use to eavesdrop," Alethia said.

Cassie was running at her top speed in a crouched position back into the dense lava vents, hoping her human outline would be obscured by the heat waves.

"Yes, Alethia. I've got it. Give me a minute to focus here," Cassie said.

"You bet."

A solid minute before she stopped running, she was now far enough behind mounds and rocks big enough for cover. Once again, the interior planet's humidity and heated air swam over her body while a salty taste returned to her dried-out nose and mouth. She stood still for a moment, bending over to catch her breath, far more difficult to do on a hot, dusty planet with perpetual shadows and a slightly less-than-ideal oxygen percentage. With less gravity than

Earth, running hard and far on Mars was the only advantage on the planet. While profoundly better inside their cavernous world compared to the changing Martian surface, the smaller percentage of oxygen, along with everything else, was more noticeable when physically stressed. It was always evident when she would see the new arrivals; the heat and the need to gulp in air was always unavoidable, followed by the soured-face expression from the smell and taste that was difficult to embrace and hide.

Cassie remained bent over to rest, then stood to scan for the place where she'd hidden her kit. It was easy to find. Mere feet ahead and covered by rocks, she extracted a heavy pack of gear.

"I'm assuming you'll be traveling light to Freeport," Alethia said.

"You read my mind," Cassie said. She chuckled to herself, anticipating Alethia's normal response.

"No, I can't. You know that joke is old," she said.

"Not to me. But yes, I will be traveling light," Cassie said.

As she spoke, she ran through her items and pulled out edged weapons for close quarters, lots of water, her own transceiver, and a makeshift poncho for camo and sleep. After a minute of looking deeper into her cache, she found a necklace made of cord where two whistles hung. Both were made from some kind of metal, maybe aluminum or pewter; regardless, they were hard to deface, durable and solid enough to create two separate, differently pitched, piercing screams.

"I see. Swift, silent, and deadly," Alethia commented.

"Yup," Cassie said.

"No long-distance arms? Bow and arrow. Rifle or sidearm," Alethia said.

Cassie nodded as she examined each tool in her kit for travel.

"I pick up some along the way or take theirs from them," Cassie said.

"I see. Old-school. What's the play?" Alethia asked.

"Track them, find them, stalk them, and kill them," Cassie said finally.

"Yep. Hemingway: 'There is no hunting like the hunting of man,'" Alethia quoted.

"Hmm. I like that. Who is he?" Cassie asked.

"A famous White man of privilege whose writing reflected patriarchal ideals, sexist, classist, and hedonistic themes about manliness. Died in 1961 after struggling with depression and alcoholism his entire life. Sad life. Clear, coherent, succinct, precise prose. Influenced great writers and American literary minds."

Cassie stopped for a moment and embraced the irony. While she could grab Hall and convince her to run away with her, she now planned to attack a group of Patrician elitists, racist men who would undoubtedly underestimate her because she was a woman and because they felt entitled to take anything they wanted.

"Hmm," was all Cassie said.

"Yep. Ironic. You're about to go all-in to fight and kill them, and they are a reiteration of this Hemingway of a bygone age. Pretty wild."

"Yes."

And with that sentiment floating in her heart and head, she started her trek with a well-paced jog.

4

...–

LEE DID his best to remain on both feet as he approached the shuttle's cockpit. Fighting the tilt, pitch, sheering, and smoke, he made it just in time to see Glenn hastily correcting his flight path to clear the crater from the devastation of the Fort Sumter garrison stood proudly just three years ago. Now, even though the crater was small by Martian standards, it was still large enough to alter the unground atmosphere. Flashes of prior planetary reports he'd read reminded him the hole created perpetual, heated winds and acted as a lightning rod whenever electrical storms erupted on the surface. Fortunately, there were no storms to create further havoc on their shuttle, but the laser blast on the starboard side did damage thrusters, and the shuttle was far from top-shelf. Lee knew that the ship had was only half fueled, but he was hoping it would be able to make it to Freeport, where they could refit it and refuel to start searching for Kurtz.

"Can you make Freeport?" Lee asked.

"We're locked in, but we're in for some buffeting from the interior's atmosphere," Glenn said without looking at him, his hands and feet manipulating instruments as if he were playing a difficult sheet of music on an archaic organ. Just as the ship passed the terminus between the Martian surface and the planet's interior, bright flashes of light and expanding red, blue, and gold ribbons from flames outside the ship ballooned around the cockpit's shields, obscuring exterior viewing. With the shuttle shuddering and dropping suddenly, standing in place without falling on his face was more of a miracle than luck.

"Strap in, Captain. We're in the shit now, and it's going to heat up. Instruments say we should get to Freeport if we don't blow up," Glenn said.

Lee moved quickly back to his seat, more out of wanting the pilot to focus on his work than fear. The ship continued to shudder while the light from the flames outside started to filter into the darkened, smoky transport.

"Are we good, Captain?" Henson asked.

"We're not dead yet, though the day is young," he said.

Lee had walked away unscathed from two shuttle crashes—well, more collisions than actual crashes—and he'd certainly had his share of turbulent space and air travel, but this was different. While the atmosphere reentry had been relatively painless, the travel, approach, and transition through the surface crater into the planet's interior was far more difficult, as if jumping from a high position into a body of water—not enough to kill immediately but enough to cause pain from smacking into a less-than-solid surface or to tear limbs. It was worse than a rocket-less reentry into Earth's atmosphere, which was saying a lot.

After more buffeting, the expanding light from the exterior seemed to wane. Lee could tell that the portside engine was working based on running lights while the starboard thrust was less responsive, the occasional electrical arching indicative of electrical surges and shortages. There were increased rapid moments of rapid drops in altitudes and sudden banking in what felt to be a semicircular pattern at times, all the while with varying degrees of deceleration and sudden braking.

After what seemed like an eternity, the braking suddenly increased, and the ship seemed to drop into a skid into the ground, jolting everyone inside with a solid bang. The interior lights flickered still dimmer, and there was more electrical arching both above in the lights and through some instruments on the ship's side. Before anyone could say anything, the shuttle's two side doors opened rapidly, obviously deployed for an emergency landing.

Lee was unbuckling his safety belt as Glenn dashed out from the cockpit, issuing orders.

"Everyone out! Grab your gear, and get some distance in case she blows!"

Lee wanted to stop Glenn, hoping for a more organized deployment, but the pilot was already gathering needed items as he moved to the hatch, then jumped outside. Not wanting to find out firsthand what being in the middle of a shuttle explosion would be like, Lee followed suit, reiterating Glenn's order, fully hoping that there would be no further damage to the ship, as it would be vital for his search efforts.

As he stood to reach the open hatch, Lee felt both the heat and humidity of the planet. He became dizzy at first, braced himself on the back of a seat, and slowed down his orders, as he was feeling short of breath. He wondered if he had hit his head or if getting up too quickly had made him lightheaded. This had become an issue over the last year, as his antiaging medication was totally gone. His weight also had increased due to a slower metabolism, remaining in orbit, and not exercising as much as he should. He thought of all the time away from Mars, wasting time, and not focusing on catching and killing Kurtz and her insurgents—it was a death sentence to him and all Patricians on the *Lee*. It was almost as if Captain

Taylor didn't care about his orders and loyalty to the admiralty and Earth.

What the hell! Fucking traitor, he thought.

Lee took a moment, readjusted himself, and made sure he was stable on his feet. The other men looked as if they were going through the same thing, some better than others —moving with urgency and then slowing down as if winded, hit with the overwhelming humid heat.

"Wow! This sucks," Henson said.

Adding to the discomfort were two discordant senses: The breathable air was uncomfortably warm bordering on hot, and a perceptible taste of salt was in the air. With all his senses under attack, Lee felt his mood decline further as his anger swelled.

We wouldn't be in this shithole if the captain did his job!

Henson recovered quicker than Lee and was already urging the other men to collect their kits and move. Lee did his best to focus and follow with some authority and dignity, even though he was struggling with the rapid change in atmosphere. He did his best to catch up with the others, who had mostly exited the shuttle while he waited, as if in the role of a captain's last man to leave the ship, and for Henson to pull a plebian woman along with him by her bounded hands.

Lee was too focused staying on his feet, straightening out his uniform, making his limbs work and exiting the ship without falling to care who the woman was. Once outside, he saw all his men several feet away, sitting or lying down on the ground with gear sprinkled around them in clumps. By the time Lee reached them, he fought the urge to drop his gear too and looked back to the shuttle to see Glenn methodically and carefully inspecting the shuttle, seemingly immune to the atmosphere and clearly focused on the ship's health more than his well-being. He had met Glenn before and was impressed that he often took on more surface missions than most. With his flying skills and knowledge of the planet and resources, he would make for an important asset.

Originally, Glenn was opposed to joining Lee, desperate to return to Earth. He'd left before his baby girl had been born and hoped to be home before she was three years old. But that was not going to happen under Captain Taylor. She had to be five years old now. Once Lee captured Kurtz and the admiralty promoted him to captain of his ship, he would make sure to promote the pilot.

Lee took yet another minute to get his thoughts in order. It was hard to think while combating an alien environment. Years of being on a ship with human-controlled environs made the sudden change difficult. The only two times he'd been on the planet's surface were in an exosuit, which made the hostile surface bearable. He looked around and saw that his soldiers were all on their asses and backs, getting their uniforms dirty.

"Everyone—to your feet," Lee ordered.

There was the smallest of delays before XO Henson echoed the same order with more zeal. Only then did the men moved quickly to their feet, fighting the heat, humidity, and air.

"Go through your kits; redistribute rations and gear. Arm up and set up a perimeter around the ship. XO—get a status update on the ship, and then pick a pair to go with you to reconnoiter Freeport's outskirts," Lee ordered.

A unison of affirmations rang out, and the men scattered, leaving Lee alone, fortunately. He could now take a minute to recover from the crash and settle in a moment of peace. Still, Lee was about to issue another set of orders to Henson when he saw him pulling the plebe behind him on a makeshift leash around her bounded hands.

"She's not going anywhere," he muttered.

Lee turned around to take in his location. He nodded as

he appraised his pilot's landing skills. He'd done a good job landing close to the far city wall, just about one hundred feet away, while far enough from the low-lying structures on the outskirts of Freeport, leaving about one thousand feet of space with perfect line of sight. It would be easy to dig trenches to face the town's only approach vector for defense and have more than enough space to launch once the ship was ready for flight.

Not bad, Lee thought. *Locate and acquire fuel and supplies from Freeport. Hunt Kurtz down. Take her head and hands for identification and display in the Admiralty Hall of Justice, and get my ship back.*

Lee became aware that someone was behind him, clearly waiting and not wanting to interrupt. It was Glenn.

"Report," Lee ordered.

"Starboard thrusters need some work. Some metal, a handful of nanites, and some Martian soil could do the trick, and we'll need more fuel. I can't guarantee the ship will ever leave the atmosphere again to orbit, but it can do recon in here," he said, motioning with his hands within the chasm. "The ship could do limited time on the surface as long as there's no storms, but it is a wonder we made it this far."

"Taylor doesn't have the guts to blow us out of the sky. He'll regret that. Weakness," Lee said.

Glenn's expression was puzzled. He tilted his head as if he had missed the point.

Maybe he's not as smart as I thought, Lee pondered.

"If the *Lee* was my ship from the start, and he mutinied, I would have blasted him out of the stars. How he and his idiots missed that opportunity is his loss and our advantage," Lee explained.

Glenn looked at him almost blankly, as if more detail was required to provide a more thorough explanation. At first, Lee wondered if his star pilot was less intelligent than he had thought.

I guess you can have skills and not be smart, Lee thought.

Finally, Glenn spoke as if coming out of deep thought.

"Oh, I was thinking that the shot the *Lee* took was *precise,* damaging the shuttle as opposed to destroying it. The portside and fuel tanks in the rear were completely exposed for a shot. Either one would have ended our flight, and that's while we were exiting the launch. My options were limited when leaving the ship as well, and we crossed their forward main guns, where I was sure we were all dead. Instead, they took an incredible shot, missing the starboard's critical main thruster's components but damaging the struts holding it together. How they did that is either crazy luck for us or skillful shooting on their part. Either way, I'm surprised we made it this far," Glenn explained.

Lee took a moment to digest the report. The answer came to him quickly.

"Or Providence, Glenn. Proof that God is on our side," Lee said.

While not a particularly religious man, he did believe that all his actions, for his family's name and heritage, admiralty, and Earth, were destined for achievement under the watchful eye of God. He was about to explain further when Henson came up on his left with the plebian woman in tow. Lee turned to take a good look at the mystery woman. While happy she was not a slave or a surf, though slaves were not allowed on the *Lee* after Taylor took over, he wondered what use this plebe in front of him could be. Hopefully, Henson wasn't thinking that she might be for entertainment or sex for his men. He needed them to focus. As he looked closer, he saw a bruise just below her right eye and her dark hair a mess; clearly, she was not selected for looks.

What the hell does she have to offer? he thought.

"This little witch was part of the survey team covering the main route from Freeport, beyond Fort Deadly and allegedly into those mountains over there, where Kurtz and her cronies are hiding. I thought she might be helpful for intel," Henson explained.

As he spoke, the plebe slowly moved her bound hands to her eye until Henson snapped them back down with a sharp yank.

Lee took a closer step and examined her. For a plebe, she was darker than expected, implying some Black blood in her. She was smaller than most, her olive-green jumpsuit covered with stains and dirt, as if she had been on the planet for some time. The material was native to Mars, making her suspect. There were some rips as well, but what stood out for him was a recent tear of an insignia of some sorts, based on the clean outline it left behind from rest of her clothes.

"Tell the captain your name," Henson ordered.

Lee interrupted, focusing on more important issues that came to mind.

"Don't care. What race are you? What was that insignia?" Lee asked, pointing at the outline.

The woman looked down and tried once again to touch her eye.

Henson pulled her hands down sharply again, allowing Lee to slap her right on the bruised eye.

The woman cried out in pain and reached for her eye again, only to have her hands pulled down violently again. Lee was about to hit her again when the woman spoke.

"Mother was Patrician and Father, surfer!"

Lee stepped back as if there was a chance of contagion. He found mixed breeding to be vile. He struggled to imagine under what circumstance such a thing could happen, except maybe through rape. His hand drifted to his sidearm.

"No! No self-respecting White Patrician would ever do that unless forced," Henson blurted out.

"Agreed," Lee said, fully gripping the hilt of his gun on his hip, truly at loss as to what good she would be to him. He was weighing if her knowledge was worth the effort, water, and time to keep her alive until they found their quarry, and he was moving in the direction of her not being worth his time. Once his hand was on the hilt, he saw Henson take a step back. Just before he unholstered his laser and raised his gun to point-blank level, Glenn spoke up from his side, stepping into the field of fire than away like Henson.

"Sir, sorry for the interruption, but I couldn't help but notice that her insignia outline looks like the MAC–SOG badge. She might not be just a surveyor, but she may have more intel on military information and observation. I've seen her a couple of times exfil from well beyond the frontier and far from Fort Deadly. That could be very helpful, sir," Glenn said.

A MAC–SOG badge put the woman with Military Assistance Command–Studies and Observations Group. A recent revival of the intelligence arm for inserted ground forces, she might have operational details about their location, Freeport, and where they would have to go. This new information about her level of competence and Glenn's proximity to his line of fire were important points to consider.

Lee lowered his sidearm back into the holster and spoke directly to Henson before turning his attention to Glenn.

"Okay. Henson—find someone to babysit her. I need you to rally the troops for orders. We'll interrogate her later. Glenn—good observation. Next time, move away from the field of fire unless you want to get killed," Lee said.

"Yes, sir. Sorry, sir. It's been a while since I've been in a combat situation," Glenn said as he stepped back and to the left of the prisoner.

"You flyboys really are something," Lee said with a smile.

Henson spoke next, clearly unhappy with the order to

keep the plebian alive after what had seemed an obvious waste of time.

"Will do, Captain. The only one who could watch her is the cook, really. I don't think he's as compassionate as you and me about her, and I don't want her near my food," Henson explained.

"Me, neither," Lee agreed.

"Sorry for the interruption, sir, but I can keep her latched to me as I make repairs to the ship. If I can glean any information out of her as I work, I'll report as soon as possible. If that's okay, sir," Glenn said.

Before Lee could agree, Henson threw the woman's leash at him, clearly happy to be done with her, as if her proximity posed a serious risk of disease. Glenn fumbled to catch it and recovered.

"Are you okay with that, sir?" Glenn asked, clearly respectful that he had not been ordered by the CO.

Lee smiled, appreciative of the pilot's deference and ideas, two skills he was happy to see in the young man.

"Yes," Lee said.

Glenn tightened up the rope around his left hand and took his right hand to unholster his sidearm, then surrendered it hilt first to Henson. Henson's look of surprise was enough for Glenn to explain.

"My back might be toward her at times, and I don't want to present any risk of her taking advantage of that and having a weapon, if that's all right, sir," Glenn said.

"Not exactly tactical, but not a bad idea. Get going, Glenn," Lee said.

"Yes, sir," he said, and walked back to the shuttle with the woman struggling to keep up behind him. It was only then that Lee noticed she was limping. That was good as it reduced her risk of running away like slaves used to do before the chemical restraints implanted in their brains.

Lee watched them both move under the heated, humid, dark light of their new world.

He sensed more than saw Henson come up from behind to watch as well.

"He's a better man than I," he said.

"For flag and admiralty. Do you believe her? I bet she has some nigger blood in her," Lee said.

"Agreed, sir. When the time comes, do you want me to put her down, or should we let him do it to reclaim some dignity? I mean, he really is giving up some of his reputation by keeping her tied to him, even if he is ordered. No true soldier could swallow that much pride for orders," Henson said.

"Yes. We should let him have that. If she was a better looker, she might be of more service, but once we get what we want, we'll let him do it," Lee said.

"Makes sense, Captain."

Lee nodded and began to think of more important things.

"Are the men in position?"

"Perimeter is nearly done. The cook has prepped some calorie-dense rations for patrols, and Conroy and Rhett are reconning the port's outskirts for activity. So far, none. It looks like they are steering clear from us. Probably a good move for them," Henson said.

Lee nodded in agreement. He was still focused on the pilot, the woman, and the shuttle sitting exposed to all to see and surrounded by his men for cover.

"Okay. We'll connect in fifteen. I want a plan to confiscate the material and fuel for the shuttle to launch in four hours and enough supplies to feed our men better. The cook is good, but some better food will help the men adjust to this cesspool of a place," Lee said.

"Will do, sir," Henson said with a nod and left.

Lee watched Henson move out toward the shuttle and encampment, glad to have a minute alone. He was bothered by the sweat running down his backside and face and found his uniform tighter and stickier than when he'd left the ship's controlled atmosphere. He took a moment to pull at his shirt and pants and wiped his forehead with his uniform sleeve.

Okay, Lee thought.

He shook his shoulders to help straighten out the material of his uniform, stood erect, and held his chin high.

"Time to make history," he said.

5

"I STEP out for five minutes to enjoy a cup of coffee on my veranda, just a moment of peace, only to see a shooting star heading to Freeport in an underground cavern. You two come in with a story of mutiny on the *Lee,* an XO gone rogue with delusions of capturing Kurtz, and orders already transmitted from my comm center for engagement with enemy combatants who may or may not have survived a crash landing. Did I get the gist of it?" Lt. Commander David Strong said.

Bennett sat just opposite Strong, with Sherman sitting on his left so he could keep an eye on him.

"Yes, Commander. That's the summary," Bennett said.

"I warned him to stand down, LT. He just got drunk with power," Sherman said in a serious tone.

"Someone had to lead, sir," Bennett countered.

The repartee was immediate and natural.

Strong contained his smile to a smirk.

"Yes, of course, Chief. Always the voice of reason. A steady hand on the tiller, I hear," Strong said.

"Like a rock," Sherman said.

"You know," Bennett said, doing his best to continue

with a straight face, looking directly at Sherman, "I did it for you. I took the lead because I witnessed firsthand you punch that same XO in the nose to protect one of your team members."

Bennett turned back to address Strong.

"I thought cooler heads should prevail, sir."

Strong's smirk bloomed into a smile.

"Yes, I do remember Captain Taylor mentioning that. Thank you for stepping in, Bennett," Strong said.

As if to refocus the men, Strong pointed to the waiting coffee decanter and cups, all Martian-made from Freeport, and waved them to take some so they could get down to business.

After a few moments of moving, balancing, pouring, and settling back, Strong got to the point.

"So, what are we dealing with? Data, fiction, and speculation welcomed," he asked.

There was a moment of silence, evident that the sincere question required a thoughtful answer, as lives were at stake.

"Well, Captain Taylor has been aware for some time that his XO has been less than pleased with how the captain runs his ship, especially the elimination of class privileges, such as having no slaves onboard, giving surfs and plebes free reign consistent with midshipmen, and all personnel treated equitably, promotion based on meritocracy. It's a benign dictatorship—the captain's rule and word are absolute—but he has leveled the field, reduced barriers, and focused on getting the best from all, regardless of status," Sherman said.

"Focused on adaptation to an ever-changing environment," Strong commented.

"That must drive the XO mad. That kind of shit develops fierce loyalty and conviction," Bennett said.

Strong nodded in acknowledgement, sipped his coffee, and waited for more input.

"Captain Taylor put out a false flag about the admiralty

being disenchanted with him and offered a Lee a chance at a commission, ship, crew, and prosperity. The only thing he had to do was seize the ship, imprison the command crew, and find and kill Kurtz," Sherman said.

Strong chuckled and took a sip of his coffee.

"A remarkably easy task," Bennett said as he looked at his right hook hand. He had thought about trying to hold the coffee cup with his hook, but he didn't want to break the handle. Such native-made cups were hard to come by, and he found when he was angry, he was less in control of his apparatus. The thing that pissed him off was less about Cassandra Kurtz using his body parts to destroy a ship and fort in one decisive swoop years ago, but the arrogance that someone who had spent all their time aboard a ship, far from planet-side conditions, could think such as task of finding and killing Kurtz was an easy errand.

"Clearly, Lee and his team have no idea what they are dealing with," Strong said.

Bennett looked up and saw that Strong was looking at him. Maybe it was a look of concern. Maybe it was an assessment of his state of mind. Bennett waited to find out.

"Speaking from personal experience, if he is anything like I used to be, he should be considered dangerous. Blind ambition will make for a highly motivated adversary. When Kurtz captured me, even though I was less than enthusiastic about my mission to terminate her command, I did get close to her. Not that I ever had a chance. If it wasn't for Hall and Virgil, I'd be another footnote in the list of those who wanted money, power, and status to kill her," Bennett explained.

"And yet you remain," Strong said.

"I think the eye patch and hook gives you mystery and gravitas," Sherman said.

Again, Strong controlled his smile to a smirk. Bennett was always impressed by Sherman's lack of reverence.

"To add, he is younger than I was, for sure. If he has a

crew of devotees, he will definitely pose more of a threat than I did," Bennett said.

Strong was back to nodding, less about agreement and more about understanding Bennett's analysis. Strong looked at Sherman for his assessment.

"Bennett is right about the XO's motivation, his crew, and the danger it possesses, but I think it will play itself out in our favor," Sherman started.

"You're thinking of his arrogance and lack of knowledge?" Strong asked.

"Absolutely. He has been to the surface maybe three times while we've been in orbit. Medication for health and youth is long gone, meaning hard work, focus, and meaningful activities are the only way to offset physical and psychological deterioration. While the captain and command crew and his team have embraced the frontier, it has made us more respectful of strengths and barriers, and I think, hardened us. Lee has no idea what he is walking into," Sherman said.

"While Mars gravity will feel great, the heat, methane, humidity, natural predators, even the lack of bright light will hamper any mission he might have in mind. I had Hall on my side, and she was trained for this kind of hostile environment. Unless he has someone similar on his team, well, they're kind of screwed," Bennett said.

"The other thing is that they left under less-than-ideal circumstances, under fire and without full preps. They stocked pile lasers and refills, but they have no idea they will be depleted due to the iron and electrostatic buildup on Mars. They definitely don't have comms for any coordinated strategies and objectives," Sherman said.

"Less firepower than expected and blind," Strong said.

"Any food and water they brought will be running out, and if they don't get a supply of treated water, they won't last five sol days," Bennett said.

"Provided they survived the landing. That shuttle was in bad shape," Sherman added.

"And we've haven't even accounted for these new sand traps and squids the Freeport people have reported, and hostile forces who don't like intruders," Bennett said.

Strong took in all the data, sipped his coffee, and remained silent. After another long pause, he spoke.

"So, if they are alive, the only thing we have to do, really, is wait five sol day. They will be dead either from dehydration, heatstroke, predators, or us natives," Strong said.

"Yes," Bennett said.

"And food poisoning might play a role too," Sherman added.

Bennett gaze shifted to look at Sherman in conjunction with Strong.

Sherman revealed a small smile before spilling the additional intelligence.

"One of Lee's mutineers is the cook, Lyman. He's a piece of work. Nothing worse than an angry cook preparing your meal. Anyone in the know knew enough to avoid his cooking. The command team and crew took turns in food preparation. Best move Captain Taylor ever made in addition to not allowing slaves on the ships. He is so bad, he didn't even notice half the crew never showed up to eat, all shifts, and never accounted for misplaced cooking material and some basic ingredients," Sherman said.

"Wait a minute. Where did you get the food stuff? Planet-side?" Bennett asked.

"Freeport. Weekly shuttles at first and then monthly with preserved, salted meat and Martian moonshine, not for drinking but for marination. Honestly, sirs, you haven't lived until you've sampled Captain Taylor's marinated beef Wellington, slow cooked for two full days," Sherman said.

"Wow," was all Bennett could say.

"I have to say, Taylor sure does have skills," Strong said.

"I know, right? By the way, he sends his thanks for the canine and rattus liver suggestion. At first glance he was doubtful, but . . ."

"Fortune favors the bold," Strong finished.

"Absolutely," Sherman said.

Bennett was smiling. Somehow, it all made sense. Bennett had come to find that the captain of the *Robert E. Lee* and the Fort Deadly commander were identical in style—respect beget loyalty, equality beget best efforts, and good food sealed unity.

Bennett heard the steps, running steps from down the short hall, and then a young female cadet, Sue Owen, about ten years old, burst into the room. She was holding a piece of paper, came to an abrupt stop, and stood at attention.

"Sirs! Report from the comms. Message intercepted from Freeport: Open transmission from the civilian militia. Source handles *KC1-WVS* and *WSIB-413* report status."

"It looks like Knowles and Olsen took initiative to scan other frequencies," Sherman noted.

"What's it say, Cadet? The content only," Strong said.

Owen took a second to catch her breath and then read the short communique.

"Shuttle vessel crash-landed within walled perimeter. Adjacent structures vacated and pulled to other end of town. All useful material pulled back with few exceptions to allow them to leave but nothing more. Will observe for now. Will engage if they persist," she said.

Owen looked up to acknowledge she was done. They could see she was resisting the urge to salute as they were at alert. Bennett was able to hide his smile. He had come to understand that such an act diminished a young cadet's sense of service and duty. Questions, however, did not, and more often, the opposite of whether the cadet could answer or not. He had faith Knowles and Olsen wouldn't let one of their own enter a room of officers unaware and ill-prepared.

"These transmissions, are they legitimate?" Bennett asked.

"I've heard them interact with Field Officer Johnson and the Third Platoon this week. Cadet Olsen confirmed comm log, and Cadet Knowles confirmed. Specialist Hall told us they've been around for years shifting frequencies all the time, but they are considered the voices and newscasters of Freeport Twelve and Thirteen," the cadet reported.

Strong extended his hand for the paper, and Owen took one step, handed it to him, and returned to position. She waited while the commander reread it, more out of habit and less out of questioning.

"Good," Strong said.

"Sir," Owen responded.

"Owen—head to the mess hall and grab something for you and the cadets on duty. It's going to be a long couple of days. Please have duty watch office set you up with cots. I want twenty-five hours' coverage. Dismissed," he said.

"Yes, sir," Owen said. She stood a little straighter in lieu of saluting and left.

Bennett was waiting until he heard the cadet leave before he spoke again.

"Is it me, or are the cadets getting younger?" he asked.

Strong answered as if he had anticipated the question.

"Most of the Freeport parents want their children to stay back here, learn and gain skills here or with the militia before they head out to their oasis," Strong said.

"Looks like Fort Deadly and Freeport are the war colleges. Not a bad idea. How long are they committed?" Sherman asked.

"Until they're twenty-six Martian years," Strong said.

The weight of time sat with them all. The young Martian

youth would learn survival skills in harsh environments and stressed resources until well in their adulthood, and only after that would they be able to head off to a far more temperate, calm, and gentler place near the equator commonly seen as a paradise.

"That is, well . . . That had to be a very difficult decision to leave their children behind," Bennett said.

He immediately thought of Cassandra as a young girl, lost for thirty minutes in the Delta Exchange where she witnessed slave auctions, physical abuse, child trafficking, and a whole lot of things no child should see for any reason. It changed her. It changed him.

"Yep. The skills they will learn and the bonds they make now will create a better future. You can't get those skills when you live in peace and comfort," Strong said.

"Speaking of comfort, set your clocks, men. I bet you that Lee and his mutineers last three days, four days tops. That excludes active engagement by Third Platoon and the militia," Sherman said.

Strong looked at Bennett to get his prediction.

"Agreed, if they are contained. I can't see them making it more than four days," Bennett said.

Strong took in the data, looked back at the communique, took a sip of his coffee, and then looked at both of them.

"Okay. Will keep your standing order of containment: Recon, scout, probe, and test. Weapons free. Deadly force authorized if engaged," Strong said.

All three men nodded. It had been a while since Bennett was part of an offensive against trained men. While there was a bit of excitement, it was less about the taste of conflict and more about a change in venue and a learning experience in armed conflict for the cadets and trainees.

As long as they keep their distance and are safe, Bennett thought.

"Will Captain Taylor be coming down to catch his missing flock?" Strong asked Sherman.

"He's supervising repairs on the *Lee,* reconfiguring the brig, and prepping transport tubes for extended cryo-sleep for transport back, if and when the admiralty should come to take anyone back to Earth," Sherman.

Bennett gave a side look to Sherman. Strong's expression also conveyed the need for explanation.

"Captain Taylor convinced the admiralty that the *Lee* should remain in orbit, under his command, as well as the other ships as a means of establishing diplomatic and commercial trade with Earth. He wants to give any crew members or anyone here an opportunity to get back to Earth if they want. So far, the admiralty agreed. Long-range scanners surveyed all vectors from Earth to Mars, from a direct approach to an attack flotilla approach, and there remains one ship en route. It's a small carrier at best," Sherman explained.

"Wow. So, the admiralty is focused on internal affairs and are leaving Mars and the rest on our own," Bennett said.

"Yeah. All reports, authorized and not, are ablaze with the massive uprising, plebes and surfs freeing slaves, and business and commerce totally disrupted. It looks like civil war has finally come. Earth is about to change," Strong said.

Bennett could see that Strong and Sherman had no joy in knowing that their home planet and their own class and society that had given them opportunities and privilege was now teetering over a cliff, about to fall, never to return.

"Well, maybe this churning will yield more equitable results," Sherman said.

"I hope so," Strong said.

The room fell silent as the men sat together alone in their thoughts but drawing comfort by being together. Considering everything that had transpired in his life before

Mars, Bennett was grateful for the opportunity he took upon arrival to Mars for his second time around, and hoped that all would work out. It did for him.

I hope it works back home, he thought.

6

"YOU KNOW, you would have loved hanging out with me back in the day," Alethia said.

Cassie felt a thin smile come across her face despite the aching legs, a knitting feeling on her left side, and an unimageable dry throat with an entirely drenched body trying to keep her cool. While she was not running anywhere near top speed, the slow jog—maybe better described as a measured trot—was maintainable, made possible by conditioning, less gravity, and her internal AI's companionship.

"I know what you're thinking—in your day and age, we would have been separated based on race, but back before the 2020 pandemic, even better, in the 2010s, we would have had a great time watching movies, reading all kinds of books with real paper, and gone to good old-fashioned parties where everyone, regardless of race, social status, and gender, could meet and enjoy the diverse company and variety of food, drink, sex, and lifestyles. I mean, it was awesome. It wasn't perfect. It wasn't free of poverty, problems, bigotry, and apartheid, but in my neck of the world, it was utopian on more levels than not . . . It was nice."

Alethia had been sitting down, leaning back on her hands, relaxed, until she moved forward to sit straighter as she spoke. Her whimsical expression, eyes gazing down at her feet, seemed to transition into darkness as she continued to talk. For an AI occupying her brain, Alethia's presentation, expression, her "realness" was indistinguishable from that another human being, the benefits of personality-based artificial general intelligence technology in the medical field. This was one benefit from Cassie's former status as an elite Patrician for which she was grateful.

"And then January 20, 2017, happened, and the slow slide into civil discord, paranoia, power grabs, and eventual fall of democracy began. I mean, sure, there were brief moments of pulling back from the brink, keeping the monster from looking back at us, but it was false hope, merely prolonging the torments with still more to come. It got so bad that simple disagreements, different viewpoints, sharing differing opinions were on par with declaring an act of war, and that was between one another, houses divided, families pulled apart," Alethia said.

For as long as Cassie and Alethia had been together, Cassie had never seen her look this close to loss and despair. In what she thought might have been close to a full day of travel from the time she had last seen Hall and the descending shuttle craft to finally clearing the dry flats and cutting through the boulder laden landscape before the so-called Land of the Giant Mushrooms, Alethia's disposition had been upbeat, positive, and focused on constructive outcomes. Cassie slowed down to stop, bent over to rest and breathe, but above all to take in Alethia's mood.

Alethia looked up from her downcast, seated position and seemed to be aware that Cassie was watching her, which she was. She then flitted out like a ghost and rematerialized in a standing position, hands resting on her knife hilts, with a sunny, confident demeanor.

"Well, enough of the melancholia. How are you doing?" she asked.

Cassie smiled again, entertained that her AI, her friend, had a moment of pain, discomfort, loss, a whole lot of emotions, and was now trying to distance herself and support her.

"Wow, Alethia. You've got some issues," Cassie said.

Alethia smirked.

"Well, don't we all. And speaking of which, why are we heading to this asshole who is dead set on killing you or, I mean, us? I mean, why don't we just pull up stakes, pick up Hall, start the great journey, and leave all this shit behind? Do you really think this guy and whomever he's brought with him will get this far? Even if they did get here, and I'm not saying they could, they'll never make to the mushrooms if they cut through the wet sands."

Cassie thought about redirecting the question back to Alethia, but it was a good question.

Why do I care about this guy? I mean, without help from the natives and Fort Deadly, Mars will swallow him whole, Cassie thought.

By now, Cassie was walking rather than just standing still. Not moving made her feel achier, and the movement helped the sweat leave her body rather than pooling on her skin. It was counterintuitive: Stop moving and heat up; move slowly and cool down despite the hot air and humidity. She tried not to think too long about it but rather focus on what was more important—self-preservation and personal happiness. Keeping a mental map of where she was in the massive maze of boulders added to the distraction from sweat and pain. If it weren't for the fact that she had traversed this land several times over the years, she would have been hopelessly lost, which still happened occasionally.

Perpetual dusk, fatigue, and no sense of time from the environment except by what she kept in your head were all recipes for becoming hopelessly lost. Alethia was right—even if enemy troops were on foot and looking for her, even if they managed to get through the other barriers, getting lost in the place of stones would end them.

"So, are you just going to ignore me?" Alethia asked.

Cassie refocused on her question. It was taking longer than expected, probably because there was no logical reason for what she was doing.

"You know, I really have no good answer except I am tired of these assholes. I know that not all of us Patricians are misogynistic, racist, elitist fucks. I mean, look at Bennett. Captain Taylor and the doctor? Men who came up in that system and were either changed by the truth or saw through it from the start. They're not all that way, but there are some that are, and for those guys, I really do hate them," Cassie said.

The vehemence of her words was as thick as it was clear. It took her by surprise. If her AI was surprised, which would have been shocking, there was no hint of it. Alethia took her typical path of logic when strong emotions eventually rose to the top.

"Do you think that if Captain Bennett had not changed all those years ago, and was still the racist individual you had hated before, and you killed him right then and there, this desire for retribution, to make things right somehow, would be less? I mean, Bennett was the last person you would have suspected to become, well, rehabilitated while on Mars. And there hasn't been anyone since. And the only thing we know about this guy is that he is gunning for you. Maybe it's just for money or a promotion or more likely power," Alethia said.

"Maybe," Cassie said.

I hate when she's right, she thought.

"You know, you have mentioned a couple of times how Bennett did change, and there always seems to be some disappointment in your voice," Alethia said.

"Okay, Alethia," Cassie said in a tone that typically translated into *Don't be a smartass.*

"It must drive you crazy when I'm right," Alethia said.

Cassie stopped in her tracks and narrowed her eyes. She closely inspected her AI, who was carefully looking over her manicured fingernails, an irrational and unlikely situation based on where they were.

Not hearing a response, Alethia looked up from what she was doing and asked, "What? Did I say something?"

Cassie was about to launch into a form of logic loop to see if her friend had always been able to hear her thoughts or if it was just that her AI had come to know her too well when she caught a whiff of something. It was a strong, pungent smell, a combination of fresh mutant dog feces, dead bodies, and damp wool somehow punching through the typical hot, salty air. The only reason she caught it was a slight shift in wind, which always occurred gradually, meaning either the source of the smell was very close or the stink was that strong.

"What is it?" Alethia asked.

"A strong smell. Hard to say how close," Cassie said.

Without thinking, Cassie looked for a boulder or set of boulders that would allow cover and height at the same time so she could hide and survey the land. While the rocks where she observed Hall were large, they were flatter, maybe two to three feet tall, allowing a prone body to hide in what little shadow was available. Here, the boulders were much taller, as high as twenty feet at some points, but consistently more like eight feet, making a clear line of sight impossible without a perch. She found her mark and instinctively crouched as she ran to the cluster and quickly ascended as quietly as she could in case the danger was deadly close.

"Wow! What a combination! It smells like the bowels of a mutant cat, smeared with the trunk of an old, soggy mushroom, if that were possible. Yuck!" Alethia said.

At the top of a boulder, she surveyed the area with her telescope, moving from eight to four o'clock. Her field of vision was confounded by a sea of similar rocks scattered all over the place and shadows casting semidarkness on ground level. Still, she noticed that at two o'clock, there looked like a long caravan of people walking in a measured narrow formation, clusters of six and eight, separated by gaps. While the formation was military, the shapes, sizes, and appearances looked more like a parade of people, maybe groups of families.

"Huh. It looks like townsfolk from Freeport are starting their journey to the Promised Land. I guess they're happy with the preliminary reports of cooler air, water, and green vegetation. Nothing like hope to motivate people," Alethia said.

"Yep. Maybe about sixty people. Looks like they got some help from Virgil Johnson's trainees based on the formation—large group for overall force, separated in smaller groups to allow for compartmentalizing losses and not exposing the entire column. They're all flanked by well-armed teams of three per group for a defensive posture," Cassie said.

"They've been doing these expeditions in waves, right? Leaving the teens behind? That's not asking for trouble – young adults without parent supervision," Alethia said.

"What could go wrong with that," Cassie added.

Cassie shifted her focus from the main group to look ahead of them, following the path the group would have to take to get through the pillars of stones.

"Based on the training we saw and in keeping with Johnson's field manual, I'm betting there is a recon team about a half a klick away," Cassie said.

As predicted, there was, indeed, a group of five people ahead of the group, all engaged with three large tentacles. The tentacles swirled and lashed out at three of the five still-standing defenders.

"Fuck! Sand squid—the recon is dealing with a squid, and the main group is heading right into the sand trap!" Cassie yelled.

Before Alethia could respond, Cassie was already leaping down to the ground and racing in the direction of the battle with her two small swords out for combat.

"Shouldn't we warn the main group first and bring help?"

"We'll do both—we'll help the fighters and send one back to warn if anyone is still alive," Cassie explained.

As Cassie ran, the origins of the foul stench became evident. Littered in her path toward the fight were carcasses of various species—mutant dogs, cats, rats, and humans—in varying degrees of decay. Some were perfectly whole, maybe even alive but paralyzed and unconscious from the tentacle spikes used to capture its prey while others were partially digested, gelatinous and half emulsified for consumption by microbes left by the squid's salvia. While no one had yet seen the body of the creature submerged in pools of wet sand, the massive tentacles implied a monstrous beast, a recent discovery in the last two years, clearly the result of Earth genetic experimentation gone wrong in the lab and then released into the Martian wilds with nanites engineering everything in their path.

What could go wrong with that? Cassie thought.

Cassie broke cover of the circle of boulders faster than she had expected and immediately jumped into action by severing a tentacle's grasp on a young woman near her, who was struggling to regain her sidearm. The woman dropped to the ground, surprised to see Cassie.

"Go! Get help! Now!" Cassie said.

With no time to celebrate or to see if the woman was on the move, Cassie was off to the next person in distress. He was fully wrapped up at the waist, but his hands were free, and he was furiously cutting at the grasping limb. While she caught the recently severed limb retracting into the sandpit, another emerged from the depths and was now lunging at her. Cassie ducked it and moved to the bend of tentacle gripping the other person and sliced at it, not enough to completely sever it but enough to loosen its hold on the fighting defender. With no time to see if the man had dropped to safety, Cassie was still moving, both hands gripping her short sword hilts as they pumped at full speed to the next victim, an unarmed woman successfully dodging the searching limb.

As Cassie bolted, there was something about the woman dodging, weaving, and deftly evading capture by two monstrous limbs, hungrily searching for her, that was familiar. Somehow, the way she moved, her presence, and appearance reminded her of someone. A person in her past.

Right before Cassie could get to her, she was grasped firmly by a powerful force around her own waist and lifted off the ground. She kept her arms away from being trapped and was able to toss one of her blades at the unarmed woman still dodging her own enemy as Cassie felt her life being squeezed out of her.

"Steady, Cassie! Hang in there," Alethia coached.

"Motherfucker," Cassie said, then she pulled her last short sword above her head, right above the limb, and pushed down with all her might. She felt the creature's arm shudder, as if shocked by the deep cut, but it did not release her, tightening instead.

Feeling her breath still being squeezed out of her, she twisted the blade in different directions to cause as much pain and damage as possible. Even as she did, she felt lightheaded, and her grip on the hilt was weakening quickly.

Cassie felt a violent motion to the left and right, as if the creature was trying to shake her to death as well. She recovered after the shaking stopped, able to breathe, although her vision was fading rapidly.

"Fuck . . . me. Sorry, Aleth . . ." Cassie muttered.

Cassie thought she heard Alethia say something, but she was slipping fast from her reality. Even though Alethia was an AI implant, she found it difficult to "hear" what she was saying at the moment. Cassie felt at first light, then numb, and suddenly very tired, as if she had reached the point of exhaustion and was finally falling asleep. With her waist being squeezed and her lungs empty of air, Cassie slipped into darkness, an empty void of black with no sound, motion, or sensation. It felt . . . restful.

7

LEE SURVEYED HIS DEFENSIVE PERIMETER, a fifty-foot semicircle around a stranded shuttle with men interspersed behind a makeshift cover facing a quiet, inexplicably near-empty frontier town. Behind them was a fifteen-foot exterior wall that his pilot had somehow managed to clear, reducing the need to defend that point. So far, his XO and two recon teams had entered the town's perimeter and had found no one. Similarly, they found very little in way of food, water, and fuel. They found some of each, but not a large cache as he had expected or as was promised by prior intel.

Lee looked back at the shuttle and was impressed to see that the pilot was still working on the shuttle. Somehow, he managed to have the plebe woman help him by holding some tools and handing them to him. It was an odd scene nearly a full day ago, about twenty hours since landfall, when she was bound and trying to hide and was now compliant, no longer needing to be bound, following the pilot around everywhere, and seemingly helpful. Lee began to rethink if her termination was necessary but then recalculated the food and water situation. He needed to make her an example of his commitment to orders and duty.

Lee turned his attention to the township edge and could see his XO and his team through the dim red hue there returning from their foray farther into the town. He was happy to see they were carrying some items, one of which looked like another container of fuel that would help reenergize and engage the shuttle's engines to function again. With plans of combining aerial grid searches with his ground teams beyond Fort Deadly, he was sure he could find Kurtz with ease.

"Bring that fuel to the pilot, boys, and divide and distribute the rations," he ordered.

"Yes, sir," they said in unison, and they nodded respectfully to Lee.

Lee waited until his men were out of earshot before getting a status update on their limited resources.

"Report," Lee said.

"Well, Captain, I am surprised. We moved deeper into the town and found no one. There's evidence that the structures were occupied at least recently, but it seems like all the occupants have continued to retreat deeper into the town's center," Henson said.

"What do you mean?"

"It looks like the structures close to the walled perimeter have been abandoned over time, leaving nothing behind. The dirt, debris and empty rooms seems like the occupants left over the time. When we moved to the middle of the of the town, the place looked more lived in, as if they were there and saw us coming," Henson said.

"A tactical retreat? Wise on their part," Lee said.

"Yes, sir. It seems like they made no effort to take all resources away from our entry points. So far, we have found some things we need like water, food, electronics, and fuel. It's as if they just up and left, not thinking about what they left behind for us. They must have seen us coming in and landing just within their walls, so you'd think they would take everything and leave nothing behind," Henson said.

"I'm guessing they didn't have enough time," Lee said.

Lee had seen official reports of caravans of colonists leaving the various establishments in search of some other place, a utopia, far beyond the mountain ranges. He never gave it much thought, but now the systematic empty exterior buildings might explain the lack of response, while the other recently abandoned structures meant that there were not alone, and hostiles were out of sight but still present.

"We found some rations, some filtered water, and other things, mostly useless. As far as electronics go, we were looking for any type of radio or communication device but found nothing assembled. There were electronic components and radio parts, but nothing I could find operational or to salvage," Henson continued.

"Weapons? Medicines?" Lee asked.

Henson shook his head.

"Nothing we can use; it looks like they are using gunpowder carbines and firearms. Old-style rifles that are holdovers from the earliest colonists' days decades ago. They dropped modern weaponry for old shit. It's in poorer shape than the ones Taylor took up, but they are the same."

"Hmm," Lee said. He continued to listen as he watched movement around the grounded shuttle. The pilot and his shadow were still moving around.

"The infirmary was rudimentary, kind of a field hospital setting. We interrupted something, though, as there was one gurney that was obviously used, blood everywhere, and some tools and flasks with a small amount of some pink liquid still inside. No idea what it was. Still, there were some food rations, water, and fuel to be had," Henson said.

Lee nodded and processed what he was hearing.

"I wonder if they are leaving things behind in the hopes

that we won't pursue them deeper, wherever they are hiding," Lee said.

"I was thinking the same thing, sir. One thing's for sure: I know when I'm being watched. Every time we've gone in, all of us have experienced a sense that someone is watching us, and they're doing a really good job of avoiding detection," Henson reported.

Lee was still listening when Henson nodded to look behind him. Lee turned and saw the pilot Glenn, waiting at attention with his recently acquired shadow, the plebe woman hiding behind him.

"Sorry for the interruption, sir, but I have an update on the shuttle," the pilot said.

"Jesus, son, have you slept at all? You look like dog shit," Henson said.

"No, sir. I'm just invested in getting the mission going, sir," the pilot said.

There we go. Someone else on the same page, Lee thought.

He had hoped to be conducting an aerial grid search sixteen hours ago, but they were still grounded. Finally, some good news.

"That's good, Glenn," Henson commented.

"Yes, sir. Thank you, sir," the pilot said.

"Okay, Glenn—what's the report?" Lee asked.

The pilot took a moment to collect his thoughts, shifting a little bit on his feet. Lee interpreted this as anxiety in dealing with senior officers.

"The shuttle is fit for launch, and while shaky, it will be able to do low-level grid searches when you want, sir. She won't break orbit again, and while we could get to the surface, I would recommend staying underground," he said.

"It's fit for aerial cavern searches. Perfect," Lee said.

"There is just one issue I will have to check out, sir, and that's the ignition fuel we've acquired to start the battery power cells.

I'm worried about the intermix of the fuel we'll be using. While I'm pretty sure the intermix is all right, if it's not, starting the shuttle could be fine or, well, catastrophic," the pilot concluded.

A silence fell over the command leadership group. The pilot's expression appeared unusually blank, even stoic. And while technically, the pilot was a lieutenant, that was in the old command structure under Captain Taylor. So far, Lee was impressed with this young man, so he was feeling okay about him being part of *his* command structure. As it turned out, Lt. John Glenn was the only officer on his team other than himself and Henson.

"Shit," was all Henson could say.

There was more silence. Lee needed to have the shuttle, but he didn't want to lose it and its pilot. As if reading his thoughts, Lee's attention was redirected back to the pilot.

"Sir, all I need to do is see if I can launch and hover for just a minute to see if she is good. Ten feet straight up, and if she's still in one piece, I can land her quick, and we're good to load up and head to those mountains where Kurtz is hiding," Glenn said.

The mere mention of the anarchist Kurtz pushed Lee to decide.

"But you could die," Henson said.

The pilot's rebuttal was swift and clear.

"Well, sir, if the shuttle blows up, you won't need a pilot, and it will take care of my baggage here. If all is good, we can get started on the captain's mission and get back home. For flag, admiralty, and Earth. Any way you look at it, it's a win for me," he said.

Lee nodded his head in approval as the young man spoke. While he was worried about losing the shuttle, he believed in the pilot's work and admired his dedication to duty and honor.

Without any further hesitation, Lee gave the command.

"Okay. You're green to go. What do you need from us?" Lee asked.

"Well, I'll need more rope to tie my baggage down in the copilot's seat and my sidearm if she gets antsy, and I think you should get to safety distance, probably just inside the exterior buildings, just in case," the pilot said.

Lee and Henson looked beyond Glenn and saw that the plebe's hands were bound again, and there was a collar around her throat. The only thing missing was a leash, and that could be rapidly remedied with rope, as requested.

Lee nodded with approval again and directed his attention back to Henson.

"Inform the men of the plan, and have them fall back to minimum safety distance behind the exterior buildings for cover. Have them fall back in threes and ensure covering fire in case those watchers become active," Lee said.

Henson was already on the move and was handing the pilot his sidearm that he'd surrendered the day before.

"We'll get you that rope quick, Glenn. Good luck," Henson said.

There was a moment of silence. It was awkward at first.

"Sir," the pilot started, "I'm sure it's going to be all right, but in case it isn't, it was an honor serving under you. You were my best shot in getting back home, and I have no regrets in taking it."

If it weren't for the fact they were in the field, Lee was sure the pilot would have saluted.

"It's going to be fine," Lee said.

The pilot smiled, turned, and pulled the plebe woman with him as he headed back to the shuttle. Even as Lee watched him walk back, he hoped the shuttle didn't blow up. It would be helpful in finding Kurtz far faster than without it. Otherwise, it would resolve getting rid of the plebe but at the cost of losing a loyal soldier. Lee had to admit the pilot was right: If the shuttle did blow up, there would be no need for his services.

Lee continued to mull over his thoughts, even though he was certain he had made the right decision. As he watched, he could see the cook handing the pilot the rope while his men retreated in an orderly fashion away from the shuttle and into the township's edge for cover and protection. Lee turned and walked behind his troops, again making sure he was the last man on the field before the field test began.

It was only two minutes before Henson's makeshift transceiver Glenn had made to communicate with the shuttle came to life, and the pilot started his launching sequences.

"Shuttle Nine launch initiated," the pilot said.

His voice was calm and firm, though there was more static on the radio than expected, almost as if the signal was being jammed.

"He moved much faster than I thought he would," Henson said.

"He's good," Lee said.

There was a sputtering of engine fire, some coughing, and then loud bangs from behind the wall where Lee and his men were waiting.

"Launch trial in three . . . two . . . one . . ." the pilot said.

There were more short explosions, like artillery shooting, causing the ground to shake faintly under his feet. Then a roar of engines erupted to life, and the wave front of engine exhaust swirled over and around the buildings Lee waited behind.

Lee released a sigh of relief. His shuttle was working and secure. He looked at Henson and gave him a thumbs-up. He could see that Henson was smiling too, probably just as happy that they did not lose a very important piece of machinery. There was a momentary sigh of relief. All was well—until it wasn't.

While the engines whined and blew exhaust from the back vent, there was a sharp sound of one laser blast, then a massive explosion. There might have been a series of explosions that followed, based on the repeated compression of air around him, but it was hard to tell due to the concussive sound that caught his ears off guard. The first sounds after his hearing returned were muffled at best.

Lee had instinctively pulled himself to the ground, close and low to the wall for the best protection from debris. He was sure everyone else did the same. They were soldiers, after all.

Lee closed his eyes and took a moment to recover.

Shit was his only thought.

8

BENNETT HAD to admit that Cadet Knowles's line of questioning was intuitive and logical.

He would have been a great interrogator for admiralty intelligence or a litigatory. Every answer given yields a corresponding, refined question, he thought.

Bennett had a momentary flashback. He remembered watching Cassie's worldwide courtroom transmission of her crimes years ago, long before she was an established interplanetary insurrectionist, no longer relegated to Earth but now an epic revolutionary on Mars, courtesy of his own and the admiralty's miscalculation of her resilience. At the time, he thought the prosecution crushed her defense counsel, not that she had a strong case, but then he noticed something the video scrubbers missed and the editors left in: She thanked her court-assigned attorney for his efforts. He was shocked then as the assigned attorney was well below her status, and the results were as expected. She was guilty. Yet still, she was kind and equitable in her dealings with him. He never forgot that and had attributed it to a fluke, not realizing at the time until he met her again on Mars that she was far more than expected.

"So, sir, Kurtz let you live, even when she knew you were hunting her down?" Knowles asked.

"Yes. Honestly, I was surprised to be alive when I awoke, minus my eye and hand, of course, but apparently, she took great efforts to make sure I survived the operation too, so that's telling you something," Bennett said.

Knowles sat in silence, obviously waiting for what that was telling him.

While Bennett sat comfortably in a small though well-padded chair that could rock, Knowles sat on a bench made for two. He was turned to face him while Owen and Olsen remained hard at work moving the dial, scanning any and all frequencies for further information on the crashed shuttle settled within Freeport's town perimeter. While the other two cadets focused on their work and Knowles asked his questions, Cadet Jefferson, a thirteen-year-old girl with a beautiful, smooth dark complexion and deep auburn hair to military length, listened in the corner, waiting for a communique to bring to Lt. Commander Strong or a duty watch officer, should the time arise.

Bennett took a moment to collect his thoughts to articulate what Kurtz's letting him live, disfigurement aside, could mean that would be useful to young minds. While it had been only twenty plus hours since the shuttle's appearance, he'd had limited sleep for fear he might miss something. He would not tolerate Sherman's teasing him if he had been asleep when something happened.

"Well, I think she figured out that I had changed. I had seen the horrors she had seen back on Earth, and I was an adult, not a child, like she was. She could tell my heart wasn't in completing my orders, and by then, Hall's and Virgil's lives were on the line. I figured if anything good came from all this, at least she would spare their lives. I didn't know that such an act was deemed as evidence of a change of character," Bennett said.

"So, she believed you? That you had changed," Knowles said.

"Yes. Through everything she had gone through and done up to that point, I guess she was still open-minded to see evidence of change. Rather than negating the new things she had learned about me, she took them at face value. I have to say, I never would have done that at her age, but then her experience was very different from mine," Bennett said.

"Do you like her? I mean, she did, well . . ." Knowles started.

"Cut me up like a piece of meat, used my parts to access a military ship as a weapon of mass destruction, and then kill hundreds of men at Fort Sumter? Yeah, that was not cool at all. But, again, I can't say I disrespect her. She targeted enemy combatants, kept civilians out of harm's way, and executed a desperate plan with long odds for success to save those whom she cared about. I don't have to forgive her for what she did to me, but I understand her motivation and respect she made the hard call," Bennett said.

Silence filled the small room. Bennett, who had been lost in his thoughts, looked up and saw that all the cadets were looking at him, analyzing him, seeing what his expression truly said about such a deep, personal event.

"Those men that landed in Freeport. Are they after Kurtz?" Jefferson said.

That question was a good one. Bennett had been thinking about it for a long time, from the first moment he'd heard about the shuttle's descent to pieces of intel from Virgil's advance elements of Third Platoon.

"Yes. I think they think that killing her will make things better for them. Maybe money, power. Maybe they think this is their way home, I don't know. I just know that they underestimated our world here. They're ill-prepared for their search-and-destroy mission, and they are totally unaware of hostile elements, human and otherwise, that inhabit this place. They are in a world of hurt, and they don't even know it yet," Bennett said.

Earlier in the day, Bennett and Sherman had met again with Strong for a stand-up meeting outside the comms center. Upon review of the situation and in absence of more data, Bennett had to revise his estimate of the mutineers remaining a viable, cohesive group from four days down to three. If Sherman's assessment of the men on the ground were only half accurate, Mars would eat them whole.

Suddenly, one of the comms came to life. Owen shifted her focus to her control pad and began zeroing in on the frequency. After some static, a strong male voice came over the speaker.

"This is Kilo Charlie One Whisky Victor Sierra outside Freeport perimeter to all with ears. Here is the following message received in its entirety relayed from WSIB-413:

"Mayday, mayday, mayday! This is Lieutenant John Glenn of the damaged Shuttle Nine from the *Lee*. Exiting Freeport heading to Fort Deadly. Just me and a plebe woman, part of MAC–SOG survey team—weapons disengaged—we are no threat. Heading in your direction. Will descend outside your threat zone. Repeat—mayday, mayday, mayday. Lieutenant John Glenn and MAC–SOG survey team member Abigail, heading toward Fort Deadly outside your threat zone. Weapons disengaged—we are no threat. Request sanctuary . . ."

The original speaker came back on the line. "Whatever's going on, that shuttle launched, blasted a hole in the perimeter wall, and took off at low altitude in the direction of Fort Deadly. Recon reports only two occupants boarded while the majority remained behind. Remains are unclear. Repeat—shuttle craft lifted off and is heading to Fort Deadly. Copy all. KC1-WVS out."

Just as the first transmission was coming through,

Bennett saw Olsen perk up and focus on his comms receiver, pulled on headphones, and listen intently as he wrote down something.

Bennett caught Owen's attention and gave him a thumbs-up to put his transmission on speaker.

"This is overwatch, Whiskey Sierra India Bravo Four One Three, inside Freeport perimeter: Shuttle craft has lifted off and left the area. It blew out the wall to clear a route. Looks like it can't get altitude and is staying low. Picked up the following traffic.

"Mayday, mayday, mayday! This is Lieutenant John Glenn of the damaged Shuttle Nine from the *Lee*. Exiting Freeport heading to Fort Deadly. Just me and a plebe woman, part of MAC–SOG survey team—weapons disengaged—we are no threat. Heading in your direction. Will descend outside your threat zone. Repeat—mayday, mayday, mayday. Lieutenant John Glenn and MAC–SOG survey team member Abigail, heading toward Fort Deadly outside your threat zone. Weapons disengaged—we are no threat. Request sanctuary . . ."

"Thirteen intruders remain behind. Appear to be disoriented and in disarray. WSIB-413, overwatch observes all. Out."

Cadet Jefferson had already snatched the two communiques and was out the door before Bennett could say a word. He was trapped in his head trying to remember if he recalled John Glenn the last time he was aboard the *Lee* so many years ago. It was a familiar name, though it wasn't from recent memory, something he had read only a year ago from a black-market book from Earth that found its way to the Martian colonies. He was still trying to remember if John Glenn was a recent person or a historical figure purged from Earth history or both when he finally realized he was the center of attention again, with all eyes looking to him for clarity. While initially surprised and wondering what he should say, the words came to him quickly.

"Well, Cadets, it looks like the intruders' lines have already broken. It took only less than a full Martian day for it to happen."

"They're not going to make it, are they, sir?" Owen said.

"No. Whatever their mission was, it's already lost," Bennett said.

9

—·—

TIRED. *So tired. Why is it so quiet? Feels . . . good.*

Cassie's mind struggled to orient to where she was. It was dark. She was calm and feeling almost . . . *rested* was the best word she could think of to describe this unusually calm, peaceful, state. She settled into the feeling and slowly reviewed what she remembered.

Watching Hall and getting shit from Alethia. Then a sonic boom of a shuttle craft. A race to Freeport, and a column of people heading toward her . . . A smell. An awful smell like decaying bodies . . .

Cassie's chest tightened, and she felt her arms and legs clench into fighting position, except she couldn't feel anything. Not feeling anything, she felt alone and feared her restful state was permanent.

So . . . this is what death is like, she thought.

"Hey, Cassie? Are you with me?" she heard Alethia say.

Cassie could feel her heart jump, and a sudden joy erupted.

A moment of silence passed before Alethia spoke again.

"Well, since your heart rate jumped and your blood pressure came to life, I guess you can hear me but can't respond. In case you're wondering, you're not dead but recovering from neurotoxin. I've been listening to the townsfolk who got to you and the others in time. Did you know that sand thing is yet another genetic experiment that has gone wrong and rogue? What were these Patricians scientists thinking? I think they were bored and wanted something new and different. Not that I'm a xeno-species specialist, but I think that thing was an originally a squid, which obviously has evolved into something crazy big and dangerous. Can you believe it, though? The rapid evolution in size and adaptation is amazing," Alethia said.

Cassie felt herself calming down, as if Alethia's presence and read of the situation was somehow reassuring. She then became aware that she was breathing, slowly, deeply, without issue. Cassie could feel the corner of her mouth turn up, a smile, she thought, which led to another thought that if she could sense this, maybe she could do something else voluntarily rather than just listening to Alethia go on about the toxin's purpose to immobilize its prey for emulsification and allow for digestion. It took some time and effort, but Cassie was able to open her eyes, which revealed an interesting scene.

"Sorry," Alethia said. "I completely missed the point. Let me bring you up to date."

Finally, Cassie thought.

Unable to move her head, her line of vision revealed people walking back and forth, casually and relaxed, though it was clear they were also armed. Unable to look up or down or side to side, she saw lots of legs and waists, mostly bare, with minimal covering of genitals only maybe for modesty, a perfect outfit for Mars's underworld. It was also clear that the legs were diverse: pale, brown, and Black, male and female, though mostly female, and very strong. These legs could be described only as muscular. Then, to her surprise, a group of smaller beings, a multiracial group of children, ran by, laughing, as if playing. It was evident that they were being chased by a doting adult, clearly having fun. Wherever she was and whoever found her, she felt safer by the minute.

"I hear this is the fourth wave of Freeport people making their way to the Promised Land. The group we came upon were their recon team that obviously got caught in the sand squid's trap. I guess they had thought they had given it a wide berth, but apparently, the squid can expand its territory from underground," Alethia explained.

Right in front of her, though a small distance away, was another person, one of the women she remembered freeing from the squid's grasp. Like her, the woman seemed immobilized, though it was clear she could now move her hands at least and seemed she was able to talk. Her vision was then blocked by two people kneeling to her level, maybe to talk to her.

"I have to say that in addition to being lucky and still alive, you were also found by two familiar faces. Wait until you see them," Alethia said.

Suddenly, Cassie spoke, surprising herself as the word came out, as she thought she was totally paralyzed.

"Who?" she croaked out.

"Excellent! It looks like some of your motor functions are returning," Alethia commented.

"Yes," Cassie said, more as a means of testing the theory than confirming.

"Do you remember Lucia and Maria? The slaves on the *Jefferson Davis* we tried to rescue? They found us. They remembered who you are. And you remember the woman who was ducking the squid's limbs? That's Sarah, the young colonist with Jacob, who found Gavin, the doctor, Nancy, and us back at the old colony. Do you remember?" Alethia asked.

A flood of memories flooded her all at once. Lucia and

Maria's awful and inhumane treatment as property—she still remembered the Patrician family name tags, Gustav and Kepler—and how her discovery and intervention made it more difficult for the *Davis* crew to continue their actions. And then, the *Davis* crew left her and her team for dead, to be ripped apart by genetically altered "pets" gone wild, but were themselves killed. She and her team were led away to their new Martian underworld home by Jacob and Sarah, these two teen colonists. It all flooded back as if it were yesterday while it had been years ago.

"It looks like you returned the favor—you saved Jacob and Sarah, and the other woman you saved got help. Honestly, you're having a great day. Maybe not with Hall and hunting, but you're alive and among friends."

"Really," Cassie said. Her voice was stronger now, and the sarcasm she wished to convey was present.

"There she is. It sounds like you're getting motor functions back," Alethia said.

An image started slowly solidifying in Cassie's inner eye. Materializing slowly, Alethia started to form into her combat-ready outfit, a compressed bottom and top with an array of edged weapons, mirroring what Cassie wore.

Cassie could now feel a smile forming. She was happy to see her friend. Before she could say anything, her vision was filled with a young woman's and man's faces. It was true. Both Jacob and Sarah from years ago were here, older, more mature with angular, muscular faces, their skins darker, firm and angular, but definitely the two from long ago who facilitated her and her team's transition from a world of privilege into a brave, dark world, a world she'd grown to respect and love for its freedom, putting the hellscape aside.

"Well, fuck me. You're right, Jacob. It's the *great* Cassie Kurtz. Who knew *we* would be indebted to *her*? I guess shit does come around," Sarah said.

Her voice was as sarcastic as ever, though it was softer,

teasing in a nice way, if there was such a thing. Similar to how siblings might tease each other in the best way to obfuscate their love and concern.

Jacob's face came into view, sharing her field of vision with Sarah now.

"I know, right? It's kind of embarrassing, though. I was hoping no one would find out that the squid caught us, but that's out of the question," Jacob said.

Like Sarah, his face was also strong and his sarcasm still active, though his eyes were soft, bordering on kind. As he spoke, a nice, easy smile came to light.

"You are quite the legend around here, Kurtz," Jacob added.

Cassie could definitely feel herself smiling.

"Cool," Cassie said, her voice stronger, though getting more than single words out was her limit.

Sarah chimed in with an explanation.

"We came across a sand squid, and your time was, well, great. We discovered these things about three years ago, and we thought there were just two of them, and not here. It looks like there are more, and they have a way of moving around under the surface."

Jacob picked up the rest of the story.

"We don't know much about them, but their grips have these suckers that transmit some drug that paralyzes people. It's kind of disgusting, but it's the first part of their digestive process after squeezing their food to death and before they puke up their stomach shit to start softening their food. Pretty gross."

"Still, recently cut tentacles stingers carry traces of the venom, which we like to get whenever we can. It's excellent for hunting and surgeries. Kills pain and renders its victim unconscious, I mean, in a deep sleep. The deepest sleep ever," Sarah said.

Jacob produced jar of pink liquid, swished it around,

demonstrating successful extraction.

"You managed to help us get six jars of this stuff. A legendary amount for one encounter," Jacob said.

"This is an unexpected bonus. I thought it was going to be a boring trip. I'm glad I came," Sarah added.

Jacob looked at Sarah and made a face.

"You had to come because I was going," Jacob said.

Sarah closed her eyes, dropped her gaze, then looked back at him.

"Hey, you might be the father, but I go where I want and when I want, Jacob," Sarah said.

Jacob put his hands up as if surrendering. This was obviously a recurring argument, maybe more discussion than a real disagreement. It was familiar to Cassie, as it had the same banter-like quality that she would have with Alethia.

Father? No way, Cassie thought.

"Whoa, Sarah. I know. I'm just saying, were you really going to stay behind and party like all the others when you're pregnant? I mean, drinking and tormenting Patties are not really on the top fun-things-to-do list in your condition," Jacob said.

The mention of *Patties* reminded Cassie why she was in the area and where she was going. The damaged shuttle's trajectory was toward Freeport, and it was clear that it was very close to the town, and that the people were not only aware of the enemies' presence but were taking aggressive action.

Before Jacob and Sarah could continue arguing, a loud blast echoed through the cavern. It was far, but it was definitely a blast, followed by the sound of a second one just as loud, all coming from Freeport's direction. The first sound was like a contained explosion, like a very rough launch sequence, while the other sounded like dynamite, not contained at all.

Both Jacob and Sarah stood up, out of Cassie's immediate field of vision. Cassie looked beyond them and could see the other woman who had been across from her was now standing with the support of two others. All were looking above to the cavern's ceiling.

"That doesn't sound good," Alethia said.

"The first blast sounded like a launch," Jacob said.

"The second one is definitely a laser blast hitting rock. You think the Patties got their ship going and went on the attack?" Sarah said.

There was a long pause.

"No. There it is. At ten o'clock, low. Just clearing the rocks, maybe twenty feet up at the most. That's pretty low," Sarah said.

"Looks like it's heading to Fort Deadly. That's going to be mistake," Jacob added.

Cassie felt she was able to lift her head up a little and was now able to see a faint red and orange glow moving at a steady slow clip, as if struggling to stay airborne, as if flying just above boulder outcrops was airborne.

"Wow. Are we headed in the wrong direction? Wait—there's no way that crew would willingly go to Fort Deadly. I mean, Lieutenant Commander Strong and Bennett are no fans of the admiralty, if they're onboard," Alethia said.

"Agreed," Cassie said. Her voice felt stronger, and making out polysyllabic words was no longer difficult.

Two sets of muscular, Black women's legs came into Cassie's immediate view. They were positioned looking and following the direction of the distant shuttle craft. Now able to look up to the torso, she could see a transceiver, larger than a handheld but smaller than a base station, slung around someone's shoulder, hugging the owner's hip.

"Mayday, mayday, mayday! This is Lieutenant John Glenn of the damaged Shuttle Nine from the Lee. Exiting Freeport heading to Fort Deadly. Just me and a plebe woman, part of MAC–SOG survey team—weapons disengaged—we are no threat. Heading in your direction. Will descend outside your threat zone. Repeat—mayday, mayday, mayday. Lieutenant John Glenn and MAC–SOG survey team member Abigail, heading toward Fort Deadly outside your threat zone. Weapons disengaged—we are no threat. Request sanctuary . . ."

"Okay. Well, this is a crazy-ass day! I'm afraid to say how nothing can surprise me now. What the hell is going on?" Alethia said.

Before Alethia could add anything else, Cassie saw one set of legs and then another turn toward her, come to her side, and then lift her up to support her. Their lifting was smooth, firm, well practiced, and gentle. Cassie was able to look to her left to see a familiar face.

"This is too much! I told you we would see her again. She's so thin, though. Not the plump girl I remember from the *Davis*," Lucia said.

The Black woman's smile and kind face was older, but she looked strong, hopeful, and had the kindest, softest eyes Cassie had seen in a long time.

Cassie slowly looked to her left and saw Maria. Like Lucia, she was older, yet still had warmth and spirit about her. While Lucia's eyes conveyed kindness, Maria's gaze shared humor and feistiness. Both women holding her up and moving her about was of great relief.

Cassie smiled and was able to utter "Thank you." It was then Cassie smelled what could only be described as urine and shit. She dropped her head and could see that she had, indeed, peed and pooped herself. A flash of embarrassment spread across her face. It was amazing that the toxins kept her from feeling herself urinating and defecating, but she could feel the rush of heat flushing her face. To Alethia's credit, she was already in embarrassment-containment mode.

"Yeah, I didn't want to mention that the toxin really relaxes every organ. It's a good thing you hadn't eaten much in the last three days. Otherwise, you would have added vomit to the mix," Alethia explained.

As if the mere mentioning of such an event could occur, Cassie felt her stomach turn first sour, then a stirring in her upper gut. A gag reflex erupted, spilling the tiny remains of what was in her gut. While mostly dry heaves, the regurgitated digestive liquid, added to the urine and feces on her legs, made Cassie feel like she wanted to die.

"Don't you worry about that at all, Cassie. This happens all the time. It looks like you haven't been eating much at all. Not much to expel," Maria said.

As if to change the subject, kindness came from a very unlikely source.

"You remember when Jacob was pricked by the squid last year?" she heard Sarah ask.

There was an eruption of laughter all around her.

"It sure as shit cleared up my constipation. That was embarrassing," Jacob said.

"No—it was impressive. Proof that from every accident some good comes out. Literally, in this case," Maria chimed in.

"Yep—clears up constipation, empties stomach, anesthetic, and sleeping aid. The squids provide a lot," Lucia said.

Cassie felt a wave of comfort, and her embarrassment eased.

"You see? It's a thing with this encounter," Alethia said.

Cassie smiled and suddenly felt tired. She started to feel weak. Soon her eyesight was graying, and she was feeling lightheaded again. She was beginning to panic when she remembered that part of the squid's medicinal benefits was as a sleep aid. Confirmation came quickly.

"Don't worry, Kurtz. You're about to fall into a deep

sleep. We'll set you up and settle you in. You'll be out for about half a day, and you should feel great," Sarah said.

Even as she spoke, Sarah's words seemed to fade as if she was moving far away. Cassie had no time to respond.

"Get some rest, Cassie. I'll be here when you wake," Alethia said.

Cassie was going to protest but it took too much energy, and she fell asleep.

10

LEE SLOWLY OPENED his eyes only to see a blurred outline of someone standing above him. Not directly above him but to the side, moving their hands and arms as if directing something. At first, there was no sound, but it slowly started to come back as he heard loud voices—orders, he thought, being yelled out. As his vision cleared, he could see that he had obviously fallen on his back and that others had somehow been up and about sooner. After a minute longer, it was clear that XO Henson saw that he was awake and offered him a hand with another person, Lyman, who was assisting him to his feet.

"You with us, sir? That was quite a blast," Henson said.

"Report," Lee croaked out, still fighting to hear, and dust and debris still falling from the sky. All of this made the oppressive heat and humidity worse in addition to a massive headache.

"We think Glenn made liftoff, but then there was a laser blast that took out the back wall," Henson started.

"Completely sheared the wall to the ground, singed dirt, debris everywhere," Lyman added.

"There are no immediate debris fields where the shuttle

was. Why he blasted the wall, and why he isn't back, is a mystery to me," Henson said.

It took Lee ten seconds to figure out what was going on. Considering the pilot's loyalty and deference to him while they had been together, he was positive the young man discovered there was some kind of danger at hand and obviously cleared the area, getting the damaged ship away from killing the others.

"Right after the blasts, a couple of the guys caught sight of the shuttle pulling away from the zone at a very low level, barely clearing those boulders," Lyman said, pointing in the two o'clock direction.

"He had to blast the wall to get clearance. Where do you think he landed?" Lee said.

Lee was rubbing his head and cleared his throat before he noticed the two men not saying anything.

"Well, I don't know, sir. I have no idea why he isn't here," the XO said.

Lee did his best to breathe in without labor and continued to move his shoulders around to relieve the tension. He pulled at his uniform to straighten it out and brush off the descending dust, dirt, and debris. The blank looks on Henson and Lyman continued.

Really? You can't figure this out, he thought.

Lee hoped they would piece it together. He was disappointed.

"Glenn was worried that the shuttle might blow up. I'm guessing something happened, and he wanted to get the shuttle as far from us as possible. Fastest way to do that is a straight line out, not up and down," Lee said.

It looked like Henson was catching on, while Lyman seemed to grasp the idea faster.

"That crazy-ass guy. You think he made it?" Lyman asked Lee.

"Probably. You saw how he flew. He's an officer of the

admiralty. He understands legitimate authority and leadership," Lee said.

By now, Henson was nodding in agreement and seemed to understand the captain's point.

"I'll send two pairs of scouts out to recon two klicks between ten and two o'clock. I bet he kept it low, cleared the boulders, and set her down. That's why there was no secondary explosion. That guy's got skills," Henson said.

Lee was happy that his XO finally got it and approved of the plan. He had now been up and walking around to where the launch site had been, which was now scorched, with walls and rock debris scattered everywhere. Lee surveyed the area in full and was pleased to see Henson already had his scouts heading out through the breached wall with water, rifles up and sidearms at the ready. With four men scouting, Lee, Henson, and Lyman at base, the remaining soldiers waited for their next orders.

This is bullshit. No more defense. We're going on offense, he thought.

"XO—send a pair of men to scout and locate a base of operation inside the development. Go deep. I want to find who's watching us and get out from the open here," Lee said.

"Agreed, sir," he said.

"I'll take one of the boys," Lyman offered.

Henson looked at Lee for approval, and he nodded. Lee was happy that Lyman had stepped up yet again to take on a mission. His cook's future was looking good, officer material after all.

Lee was already on to the next steps. He figured that Glenn was probably two kilometers at the most away, so he was hopeful that at least one set of scouts could lay eyes on him and confirm. It was possible that Glenn had to swing outside of the projected search pattern too, which would add time to find him. This was something Lee was not happy about. In either case, sitting exposed in an empty debris field with a breached wall didn't make any military sense. Lee was deep in thought when he heard his XO clear his throat.

Lee looked up and saw Henson reconsider for a moment, then ask his question.

"You don't think Glenn abandoned us, do you, sir?" Henson asked.

While the thought had briefly crossed his mind, it was easy to see that Glenn was a team player, loyal to the admiralty and rightful captain of the *Lee*. Further, Glenn had demonstrated skills and talents to keep Lee and his men intact and kept hope alive. Lee could tell a good man from a bad one. Judging character was easy when you knew where to look—if words and deeds aligned, a man's character was true, Lee had always believed.

"I am positive he's waiting for us just beyond those boulders. Once our scouts get back to confirm, we can move out in the morning. I'm planning on staying here one more night, so I want a base of operation inside the perimeter. Once established, and if we come up empty-handed when we head in, I want two men to go deeper into town to find more kit, especially water and radios. We won't last long if we don't have water or a way to purify what we find, and we'll need shortwave for when the admiralty shows up. Sound good?" Lee said.

"Excellent plan, sir. We're on it," Henson said.

Lee was glad to see his XO move off to make his plans happen. While initially disappointed that his XO couldn't see the bigger picture, he could understand why there might be doubt. And with Henson off being busy, Lee could now roll his aching shoulders and focus on breathing with ease. Gulping in the humid air, the oppressiveness of the heat, and the perpetually dark environment made for less-than-ideal transitions from ship to field command. His uniform was feeling bunched up, damp and sticky, but there was no way he and his crew would be out of uniform.

Still, the constant twilight, persistent red shadows, and the weight of darkness all seemed endless, heavy and pervasive. While there had been some hiccups, Lee could see that, in the end, he would find Kurtz and end her influence. He would accomplish where so many had failed.

"It all starts tomorrow," he said.

Lee took a moment longer to compose himself, straighten out his uniform again, and make sure his firearm holster was set to rapid release. He had no thought he would need it, but a true soldier is always prepared. When he turned, he found one of his men waiting, obviously an escort, to bring him to the town's interior. Lee was happy with Henson's foresight.

"Let's move, Conroy," Lee said.

"Absolutely, sir," the young man said.

Lee moved with both authority and efficiency. The authority piece was easy, but moving without hyperventilating and overheating was. He would periodically stop and look at something that caught his eye to recover, without it looking obvious. Much of this was not for show—this was the first time he had moved into the interior of the township himself, and there were many things he had heard of but had not seen firsthand.

For example, he had noticed that there were a handful of structures that had doors and all the windows open. All structures were about three to four stories, and the interiors that he could see were small, simple, and Spartan, with little by way of furniture—simple chairs, tables, benches. There were a few structures that towered by comparison, but they were maybe double the size of most buildings. Further, all the buildings he came across had little by way of personal items, tools, implements, entertainment, clothing, bedding, and any luxuries such as dishes, glassware, or fabric. It was as his XO had described—the place was abandoned. No personal effects, tools, or useful items left behind.

The farther they pressed on, the emptier it got. Three- to four-story buildings, all made of Martian soil via nanobots with some significant handmade additions lined the route inward. It became narrower, with more choke points and kill boxes than Lee liked. Still, he trusted his scouts and men to navigate anything the natives threw at them. With enough signs left for his scouts from the rear to follow when they located Glenn's shuttle for evac, Lee was feeling a little better when they came to what looked like a town market. It was open, with empty booths, a small number of tables and chairs, but it was the first common area for a crowd that Lee had seen as they'd traversed the town.

Just ahead, he saw the two scouts flanking the exposed area, remaining perfectly still. Henson had already stopped the group with a closed fist and had them scatter for cover while he held the middle ground, even though he was exposed in the middle of the narrow street. Lee was grateful for the stop to get his breathing and overheated body in order, but he was now growing impatient, waiting for the unmoving scouts to break cover and report. It was obvious that his XO was also frustrated with waiting, so he advanced to the right flank to talk to the scout.

But before the XO could reach the scout, he suddenly stopped and grabbed at his neck.

"Shit," he heard Conroy say from behind.

Lee turned and saw that his escort was also grabbing his neck. Suddenly, he saw a small dart smack into Conroy's neck on the other side.

With no time to spare, Lee backed away, behind a small wall. He looked back at his XO and saw him struggling to stay on his feet, then fall to the ground. Beyond him, he saw the other scout unceremoniously fall over. It looked like his tethers that held him in place gave way. In front of him, two other men yelped out in pain.

"Fall back—now!" Lee ordered.

He didn't have to give the order again. Two of his men turned in place and jumped to a dead run, passing him without regard for defensive maneuvering or order. They made it five feet beyond him before he saw them get hit with looked like a swarm of darts hitting their backsides.

Lee was still stunned, shocked how quickly his men broke rank, and how his troops went from a tactically effective squad to just him left, with none of them getting one shot off. The whole scene and situation totally surprised him.

With no time to think, he felt a pierce at his own neck, then another and another. He instinctively grabbed at his throat and stood up, as if the act of standing would help.

It did not. Instead, it made him dizzy, and he felt the ground rush to his face. It was fast.

Fucking savages, Lee thought before drifting off into unconsciousness.

11

"NOW, from the top: In what alternative universe would you think mutiny would be a viable approach to get back home?" Chief Engineer Sherman asked.

Bennett watched the young lieutenant nod and continue looking down at the table that separated the two men. Bennett felt bad for the man. While appearances could be deceiving, the interrogation revealed several things in less than four hours. He was, indeed, John Glenn, the pilot who miraculously landed a significantly damaged shuttle, fixed it, got it fly once again, and almost made it to Fort Deadly before it crashed once again. He was also the same man who put his life at risk by protecting, rescuing, and conveying a woman caught in the crossfire of a botched mutiny when it would have been easier not to do anything. While Bennett and Sherman were dubious of this report at first, it was his low-key report and the woman's emphatic and emotional gratitude that stamped that data point as accurate. Finally, when the Freeport civilian militia group found them, he immediately surrendered, asking for sanctuary for the woman. He gave no resistance to his captors and cooperated in the long march to Fort Deadly for detainment.

"There is no reason, sir, but just an excuse. I was desperate to get home to see my wife and baby again. I compromised my morals, put my faith in a false leader, and I violated my oath to this uniform," Glenn said.

By now, Bennett knew his response by heart. It had been hours since he, Sherman, three armed guards, Knowles, and Jefferson had gone over the after-action report. While the room was big, it felt claustrophobic. It was below ground, silent, with dim lights, three chairs, and a small desk. Everyone seemed to stand and sit tall except for Glenn; his flight suit was dirty, dusty, ripped at some points. His hair was in disarray; his pale skin looked sickly, but it was his countenance, that downward, wished he were dead look, that made Bennett feel bad.

Throughout the interview, Glenn had been consistent in his reporting, even when purposely misdirected by Sherman or offered a way out via an excuse. Bennett was impressed that throughout the interview, Glenn never spoke disparagingly of Lee or the others, nor put himself above them. Even when Sherman pointed out that he was an officer and might have been "mislead" by the enlisted men and Lee, the mastermind, Glenn reported that his commission demanded that he "should have known better." Bennett had experienced and conducted a few military and civilian interrogations before, and he was feeling hard pressed to see the young, disgraced officer as duplicitous, conniving, or stupid. His actions were desperate, and his thinking fell short of logical at the worst time and in the wrong place with the absolutely wrong people.

But then, people do stupid things when they're desperate, Bennett kept thinking.

"So, the only thing you can say is that you made a career-ending, colossal mistake, realized it was a terrible lapse in judgement, gave up, and returned to face the consequences, which for mutiny, is imprisonment or capital punishment," Sherman said.

Bennett could see that while the young man was shaken by what was said, he continued to look down at his folded, bound hands resting on the table, just as they had since he'd sat down hours ago.

"There is nothing I can say that will sugarcoat this. I broke my oath, made a mistake, and am willing to pay the price. I wish I had more of a defense, but I don't," Glenn said.

Bennett was impressed with how well the young officer handled himself. Sitting there, watching him unflinchingly acknowledge his mistakes, was something Bennett wished he could say he would have done at that age. It took him an entire career to come to find out the truth and realize he had been living a lie, and even back then, he had the carrot of promotion and reinstatement while this young man had just punishment, whether it be imprisonment or death.

"Lieutenant Glenn," Bennett said.

Bennett was surprised how low his own voice was and even surprised when he spoke. He had not said anything at all, letting Sherman play "bad cop" the entire time, waiting for the perfect time to pull the "good cop" approach, but the need never came. Glenn had not presented any discrepancies, questions, or subterfuge that would have warranted the approach. For all intents and purposes, what the young prisoner was reporting appeared to be fair, accurate, and truthful.

"Yes, sir," Glenn said.

He looked up briefly to confirm that it was him talking and then looked back down at his hands.

"Can you tell me a little bit about your child?" Bennett asked.

A thick silence filled the room. A simple question seemed to increase the air pressure to a crushing weight, and without looking around, Bennett knew his question, the only one he had asked in four hours, had changed the entire atmosphere.

Bennett felt the shift, experienced the weight of questions, some heavier than others, but he kept his eyes on the prisoner, who seemed to shrink further into himself.

The young man's head hung lower, and his folded hands tightened. Then a flood of tears, wailing, erupted all at once. It was startling how fast and abrupt the crying fit emerged. Bennett could tell that there had been a driving force, and while he had few details on why the pilot wanted to get home, he knew it was about getting back to a new marriage, a young wife and a child.

He wanted to reach out and comfort the young man. Knowles step forward, but Sherman pulled him back and pointed him to return to his position.

The wailing continued despite Glenn's best efforts to stop. Far from the hardened prisoner of war, a stoic military criminal on trial, Glenn did his best to form words and make sentences, but the tears, sniffling, and crying kept interfering with his attempts.

Bennett sat quietly and waited. Both as a captain and an older man, he had come to understand the wisdom of just sitting in silence. This had become particularly important to him since taking permanent residency on Mars.

Bennett had no idea how much time had passed before the pilot was more composed. Maybe it was ten minutes, maybe fifteen. In the end, Glenn's flight suit cuffs and binds were soaked, as was his chest, his eyes completely red and face blotchy from the emotional outbreak.

The silence was punctuated by Glenn's sniffling to clear his nose, but it was finally broken when he spoke again. Quiet at first but firm.

"It was after I woke from cryo when I found out I was father. The last picture I had before comms blackout is her as a baby, about six months old, maybe. She's . . . tiny and beautiful," he said.

"You know you can never go back to Earth to see her again," Bennett said.

Bennett heard a sharp intake of air from behind. He knew it was from the cadets in the room, more likely shocked that their superior officer would say such a thing, a hurtful thing, to another person who was grappling with the very thought that drove him to madness.

Glenn nodded his head in agreement and laid his head down atop of his folded hands for support.

"When Captain Taylor comes to bring you back to the *Lee*, you can never be trusted among the crew again. You'll have no place there. And if he sends you back, the admiralty will have to address your actions, and you know how that will go," Bennett said.

"Yes, sir," Glenn said.

"And it is obvious that executive officer Lee and his troops will not last the next two days on Mars, let alone survive to return victorious to Earth," Bennett said.

"It is your proverbial no-win scenario," Sherman added.

Bennett looked at Sherman, and he could see that he knew where he was going, just by the change in tone, cadence, and volume from the last four hours.

Glenn pulled his head up from his hands, readjusted himself in his seat to sit taller and look straight ahead.

"Yes, sir. That is true, sir. Understood, sir," he said.

Glenn's voice was devoid of pride, hubris, or complaint. They'd never emerged throughout the interview, and they remained absent all the way to the end.

The silence in the room returned to its weighted feel, no longer a crushing weight, but simply heavy. Bennett allowed it to sit like that for more than a minute. It was Sherman who broke the silence.

"All right, Lieutenant Glenn. You are to wait here until

Captain Taylor comes to convey you back aboard the *Lee* for further action. You will remain under guard at all times. You will comply with all requests, demands, and orders, regardless of rank, without question," Sherman instructed him.

"Yes, sir," Glenn said.

Sherman then directed his next set of orders to the three armed guards.

"Guards—maintain suicide watch. Eyes on all the time, no deviations. If this guy shits, I want one man on and two men watching. It is Captain Taylor's prerogative to determine this man's fate, and I won't allow the prisoner to preempt that with a successful suicide."

The guards affirmed in unison.

Bennett took that moment to wave Knowles and Jefferson closer to give them their own instructions.

"Bring him some food. Finger food only with no utensils. Bring water but in a soft travel pouch only. Make sure the food is protein dense. You two got it?"

"Yes, sir," they both said, and without hesitation, they were off and running.

Bennett turned his attention back to Sherman, who was now addressing Glenn. For Glenn's part, he was better composed, looking straight and compliant.

"You're not going to be a problem, are you, Lieutenant?"

"No, sir. I will follow all directions without hesitation and resistance, and wait for Captain Taylor to arrive," Glenn said.

Without another word, Sherman and Bennett got up, exited the interrogation room, and walked in silence until they had ascended the stairs and emerged in the open air. Bennett had a fantasy that upon exiting from underground, Mars's underworld would receive him with a cool, dry breeze, fading twilight, or dawn, and a fresh, oxygen-rich air to breathe in deeply. It was a wonderful fantasy. Mars was none of that. While the lighting was poor in the room, Mars's surface was not much better, though the underground did feel slightly cooler than it was above.

"So, what do you think?" Sherman said as they walked.

"I think he made a very poor decision in a desperate attempt to get home to see his wife and child. Honestly, I wish it was something more sinister, compelling, a feeble attempt to gain favor and find excuse to be absolved from his mistake," Bennett said.

"Instead, an honest kid, making an honest mistake so he could get back home," Sherman said.

"And now, he can't have either. This sucks," Bennett said.

"It sure does," Sherman agreed.

As the men walked, they saw Cadet Owen running toward them, obviously carrying a communique from the comms center. She came to a skidding stop and handed Bennett a piece of paper.

"I have to get that to Lieutenant Strong, sir, after you're done," she said.

"You bet, Cadet," Bennett said again, doing his best not to smirk at all but to convey her the same respect he would give any officer.

Give respect, get respect, he thought often these days, especially as the unofficial leader of the cadet pool.

Bennett read the short note and reread it again just to make sure he read it right. It should have taken seconds, but there was a lot to digest and more to understand. He was grappling with the question why until he remembered he was still holding the communique. He then folded the note and handed it back to Owen to continue her run.

"Good job, Cadet. Carry on," Bennett said.

Bennett stood still and watched her take off. He didn't give Sherman time to ask what he read but simply summarized.

"Virgil caught a pair of scouts, and the civilian militia has contained another pair and will bring them to him" Bennett said.

"Well, that's good news. It looks like I'll win the pool of three days max very soon," Sherman said.

"Yep. But that's not the interesting part," Bennett said.

He continued walking to comms just waiting for Sherman to ask. There were times like these when he enjoyed having something over his friend. It was a tiny thing, but it was enjoyable.

A half a minute, maybe just short of a full minute of silence, persisted until Sherman broke.

"You know, as soon as I get to comms, they'll tell me," Sherman said.

"Yes. Yes, they will," Bennett said.

Bennett waited. He knew it wouldn't be long.

"You can be so petty sometimes," Sherman said.

"Yep. Comms is over there. We'll be there . . ."

"Ugh. Okay. What?" Sherman asked.

Bennett spoke fast. He wanted to see Sherman's response before anyone else did.

"Virgil said Freeport was obviously having a massive celebration at the far end of the town. The sky above was lit by some kind of bonfire. There were celebratory gunshots, the entire section smelled of meat, which was driving his platoon crazy, and there was music," Bennett explained.

Sherman stopped in his tracks. Bennett took two more steps and turned to get a full view of his partner's expression. It was worth it. Shock melted to disbelief and then back to shock.

"What?" Sherman said.

"The good town's folk of Freeport, probably their young adults remaining until they can leave with the others, are either luring or already took down Lee and all of his men. They didn't need Virgil or us to do it, either," Bennetts explained.

More time passed before Sherman could speak.

"You are bullshitting me," Sherman said.

"I know. Not that I'm a military genius, but I would assume that Freeport neutralized Lee and his crew and are celebrating. Or it's a ploy to get them to where they want," Bennett said.

"Either way, this is just embarrassing," Sherman said.

"Yep. From one officer of the admiralty to another," Bennett said.

12

CASSIE FELT herself slowly waking up. Before she could open her eyes, she swore she smelled something, an aroma she had not experienced in decades, maybe since childhood.

Coffee, she thought.

The smell grew as did a voice that became more audible. It was a voice that seemed to be transmitted, as if it were coming over a radio or video feed. With the smell of coffee and the voice, familiar for sure, she looked in her mind's eye at what appeared to be a video feed, an interview or at least someone talking into a camera.

Alethia? What? she thought.

This Alethia looked beautiful, not to say her AI did not, but this one was striking. First, her face and features were full, curvy and soft, a vast departure from her AI image that was athletic, more on the slim side, with not an ounce of fat and far from soft-looking. This Alethia had flattering makeup, so well applied there was no trace it was in place, with perfectly almond-shaped blue eyes, long lashes, and long, braded thick hair. Her nose and mouth were full and balanced, and the lipstick and eye shadow perfectly matched her darkly layered blouse and scarf. Her blue eyes stood out and enhanced her mocha-colored skin, smooth, youthful, and completely unblemished.

This Alethia, while clearly a prototype of her AI, was a younger, untouched, even innocent-looking young woman. Her presentation looked serious, carrying a bit more gravitas than expected, especially compared to her AI, who had seen everything from death, slavery, and destruction on a large scale. Still, this one looked as if she was serious about something.

Cassie shifted from analyzing Alethia's appearance and expression and focused on an off-camera voice that was asking a question.

"So, Dr. Martin, you have the last word: Based on the discussion with your peers here, what do you think is next?" the interviewer said.

There was a pause, something her AI would never do, before she answered.

"This is no longer a slippery slope we are on. It's a cliff, an abyss, and we're the monsters looking back," she started.

She was interrupted by a male voice off camera to whom she did not look at but clearly heard.

"Don't you think that's a bit dramatic, Dr. Martin? You liberals always promote fear," the voice said.

The Alethia in front of her continued, ignoring the temptation to be sidetracked.

"We have allowed our First Amendment rights of free speech and protest to be crushed, so much so that my fellow gun owners have tacitly surrendered our right to bear arms," she started.

"That was months ago," the male voice said.

Undeterred, this Alethia continued as if she'd heard nothing.

"When is it all right for the federal government to make the excuse that law-abiding citizens who legally own and carry firearms should expect to be shot and killed when they protest? Where is the outrage from fellow Americans who support gun ownership? Where is the response from my Second Amendment peers to an overstepping federal government trampling our right to bear arms? What's next? Unlawful search and seizures? Does it now mean that if you show up with a lawfully owned firearm, expressing your right to free speech and assembly, you 'have it coming' if federal officers round you up, find you, and shoot you while you're on the ground? We're all okay with that?" Alethia said.

"So, what you're saying is . . ." the male voice started, but Alethia cut him off as if he wasn't even speaking.

"That if you are a true American who still believes in our Constitution, and don't see it as a pesky, administrative barrier that gets in the way of a weaponized, federal government, you should take your balls out of your purse, find your voice and gun, and do your duty as a United States citizen before all our rights are gone. Gaze long into the abyss, because the abyss is looking back at you," Alethia said.

Cassie felt her heart rate jump, as if she was startled. She knew her AI had an attitude, opinions that she was eager to share with her, no matter how harsh. But this Alethia, soft, polished, and clearly never missed a meal, was strong, charismatic, and did not suffer fools well. Based on what she was saying, this was right before the Great Change, when policy shifted, and the Patrician class was in its infancy.

Wow. She was pretty ballsy back then, Cassie thought.

By then, pandemonium erupted off camera with raised, angry voices, men and women. All the while, Alethia remained still, unfazed and laser-focused. Slowly, her image, the smell of coffee, and the video feed subsided, and Cassie felt light, as if floating.

When she opened her eyes, she discovered she wasn't far from the truth: She was floating four or five feet above a crowd of people, frozen in various positions of movement. Some were pointing. Others held firearms, both handguns and rifles.

"What the hell?" she said.

Cassie took a step back, barely a foot over a sea of people all converging on a center point. She saw most of the crowd was nonuniformed, men and women of all different ages, a kaleidoscope of races, cultures, and ethnicities. While she knew Black, brown and White, she had to remember the cultures that had long since been pushed into extinction, wholesale genocide.

"Chinese? Asian? Wow," she said.

Chapters of world civilization had been redacted, reduced, and completely eliminated. Ancient cultures that existed at the end of 2030 had long since perished by the time she was born. There were surfs, plebes, slaves, and Patricians, but those who were of Asian descent, East and Far East Asian, Indian—they were all gone, based on what Alethia had told her.

As Cassie looked down, her vision stretched into the distance, where she saw another person hovering above the crowd, looking down at them. Cassie felt that yelling out to the person, a woman with a dark complexion, would be too disruptive, as it was quiet in this space, a silent, frozen picture. She "walked" to the woman, who looked just ahead and below her, with arms folded over her chest, or at least that was the appearance from her angle.

While it didn't take long to reach the woman, Cassie could see that the crowd was getting denser, pushing in on a smaller crowd that seemed to be taking a defensive perimeter around someone she could not see. All the while, Cassie saw things she had seen only in old pictures: wheeled vehicles, a few official, and trucks here and there. Two were red and looked as if they were medical, while others were similar in design but in different colors with blue and red lights.

The smell was a combination of smoke, sweat, and gunpowder. The overall gestalt of the scene could only be described as anger, fury, disdain, and hatred.

The closer she got to the woman, the scene thinned out, and it became evident that there were two clear demarcations in the circle of people. The larger group surrounded the smaller group, who surrounded two or three people. The frightening part was that parts of the larger group facing the defensive smaller group had an array of firearms pointing at them. This larger group wore nothing uniform or consistent, and the people, men and women, younger than her but not by much, appeared to be of different races, more than she had ever seen. Cassie counted at least thirty-five individuals with weapons pointing at the smaller group, who numbered about twelve.

The smaller group, by contrast, was all men, bearded, faces covered, wearing tactical clothes and body armor that Cassie had seen many times when reviewing weapons and uniforms of past conflicts. Unlike the crowd surrounding them, this group was White. Whether they were Patrician or not was unclear, but they were racially the same.

"It's going to get ugly in just a minute," the hovering woman said.

The voice was like Alethia's, and the way she stood, the stance with her arms folded, was all too familiar. This was the Alethia she knew, her AI that she had come to know and genuinely love as a sister. She was an echo, at best, from the one she had just experienced being interviewed. The hairstyle was also something she had seen Alethia wear before, but the clothes were different, casual, loose-fitting. Her dimensions were not athletic but not as soft or pleasantly plump as the one earlier, Cassie thought.

"Alethia?" Cassie asked.

"Yes," was all she said.

Cassie felt odd, almost hesitant to talk to her. This was Alethia, but not the one she knew. This wasn't her engaging, affable, and relentlessly energetic AI that haunted her waking moments. This person was somber, grounded, real.

"What is this place? What's going on?" Cassie asked.

Alethia didn't answer immediately but moved closer to the center of the smaller group. In the middle were one Black man and a Black woman, arms bound behind their backs, kneeling over another person, a woman, who appeared to be injured and unconscious, at the center of this clash.

Cassie, still hovering over the conflict, now could see that the prone figure was the woman hovering with her, Alethia.

Cassie felt her chest tighten. A rush of adrenaline flooded her as fear overwhelmed thoughts. Cassie steadied her breath and looked closely at the firearms each opposing group was clutching, and two key things came to mind. In addition to the catastrophic risk of collateral death from crossfire alone, all armed combatants had their fingers on the triggers, and the three individuals at the very center might survive, as they were on their knees and lower.

"Wow! Wait! What's going on here?" Cassie asked.

By then, the hovering Alethia rose an additional five feet above the crowd. When Cassie got close to her, Alethia bent down and pulled her up to her level with minimal effort.

Now, they were both on the same level, farther from the center with a clear overview of the armed conflict and beyond. Puzzled, Cassie looked at the massive crowd's edge and could see they were in a contained area in what looked like a city center, surrounded by buildings abutting a road where she had originally arrived. Outside that perimeter, there appeared to be audiences, spectators, and what looked like old-fashioned audiovisual comms.

"Boston City Hall, April 16, 2026, or 2027. It's hard to say. It's been a while since I remembered this," Alethia said.

Cassie turned her gaze back to Alethia, who remained focused on the crowd below. The woman's voice was grave, clinical, and emotionless all at once. This was not Alethia she had come to know, who was a woman, or the AI representative of a woman of action, clarity, and focus. This person looked like she was a witness to a crime she had experienced over and over again.

"I wrote an op-ed for *The Boston Globe* and did an interview with the bright idea that should federal forces come to Massachusetts to take legal immigrants, we should all show up to represent both out First and Second Amendment rights under the Constitution, and stand our ground against an overreaching federal government," Alethia said.

Her undertone was harsh with sarcasm, deep-seated and directed inward, not out.

Cassie thought back to the time recently when Alethia appeared dark, almost brooding, and it was all about when she thought everything she considered good went sideways.

"Is this this January 6, 2021? I thought you said it was April just now," Cassie said.

"Nope. This is April 16, four or five years after the Insurrection, when the forty-fifth president returned as the forty-seventh president, and a shitstorm of far-right policies erupted on the scene. No, this little outbreak is a result of a young, morally outraged, pissed-off wife of a legal immigrant man who reached a boiling point and brought pen to paper, words to an interview, to start a war that would hasten the rise of the patriarch," Alethia said.

A blast of noise exploded from below. There were hundreds of yelling voices issuing demands to lower weapons, threats, and then gunfire. The high-pitched screams, secondary shots, yelling, and hundreds of people running away, crashing into anything in their path—everything below all erupted all at once. The flash of gun discharges faded, and more screams and approaching sirens wailed. Cassie saw the inner circle of men were all down or falling down, and the other side had more than half standing. There was sudden movement on the side still standing: One group walked over to remove the weapons and pull aside the dead and fatally injured defenders while a small group of men came to the prone Alethia's and the others' aid, checked to see if they were all right, and then removed them from the scene. As they retreated, the larger group took their own injured and dead away, leaving the smaller group in place, stripped of their weapons, gear, and face masks. All this occurred in what felt like seconds.

In the end, Cassie's attention was caught by someone writing on the ground. It was painting spray of some sort. While the movements were rapid, the print was big and bright yellow: *GO HOME, ICE. DON'T COME BACK.*

"*ICE*? What is that?" Cassie.

"The face of the bad guy at the time. Immigration and Customs Enforcement. Like I said, I suggested that we all get together to express our rights of free speech and to bear arms to a group of idiots sold a bill of goods that they were doing the right thing. We should have focused on the puppet master pulling the strings," Alethia said.

A sudden flash blinded Cassie for a moment, and when it dissipated, she found herself with Alethia again, standing right above the chaotic scene, again frozen in time but at the point where violence was poised to happen.

Just as before, everything played out again. Another flash, and it all started anew. Cassie was speechless each time it happened. She would look at Alethia and saw that her eyes were both empty and sad, her expression vacant. After another flash, maybe the fifth or sixth, Alethia stopped the process from progressing immediately as it had before.

"You should go now. It doesn't changer much," Alethia said.

Cassie was embarrassed to be glad to hear this news, grateful the horrific scene would end for her. At the same time, she wondered how she could "leave," per se. Another question came up first.

"Why do you do this? You've been watching this for a long time, right? Why?" Cassie asked.

Alethia looked at her in silence. For the first time, she seemed like she was thinking outside of what she was experiencing.

"I never worked it out, this trauma. It never left me even when I thought I moved on, got old, died, passed my brain on for AI testing and configuration. Nope. It haunts me to this day," she said.

There was a sudden flash, but instead of returning to Alethia and the perpetual review of a past moment in life, all was dark.

Cassie felt her eyes slowly open, and she felt some clothing on her that was different from her own. She was lying down, somehow pressed between three stones. As she sat up, she saw that her positioning was elevated. The space she occupied was large enough for her to lie down by her satchel and her own clothes, tightly folded, with a long tube and an array of darts opened in a leather case, all lying neatly together.

Cassie looked down and saw she was wearing a loose-fitting top—a halter, actually, with an exposed midriff—and a skirt, clearly not her style and not hers at all. She was glad to see that her sandals were still on her but wondered how and why she was dressed the way she was and where she was. As she looked up, she noticed a quick canopy had been made utilizing the tarp she had packed in her gear. She edged out from under the tarp and sat over the edge of a ten-foot drop. Right below her were two half-consumed bodies from a mutant dog and cat. The stench was overwhelming, surpassing the sulfuric stench Mars could push out at a moment's notice.

Cassie sat for a moment and assessed the situation.

"Change of clothes, positioned ten feet above the ground with the smell of death at the base, and a canopy cover to keep those mutant bats and cats away . . ." Cassie said.

"It kind of looks like your caretakers set you up to be safe but had to leave. How are you, sleepyhead?" Alethia said.

A broad smile came over Cassie's face. She was so happy to hear her friend's familiar voice. It was positive, thoughtful, and engaging, with a can-do sense and optimism she had not experienced with the other Alethia.

"I am so glad to hear you. How are you?" Cassie asked.

Alethia materialized on her optic nerve, and she looked as she remembered—short-cropped hair, an athletic small frame, with an array of edged weapons and now a long blowpipe and similar attire to what Cassie was wearing: a loose-fitting top that covered her chest but kept her shoulders, arms, and navel clear, and a loose skirt, far from tactical but functional, and far from compressed.

"Huh, you're glad to hear me? How long do you think we've been out?" Alethia asked.

Cassie took a moment to collect her thoughts. She had no idea how long she was unconscious. And while she was warned she would have a deep sleep, she wondered if Alethia had any inkling of the time lost and if she'd experienced the same dream she did.

"What do you remember? I just drifted off to sleep, after I shit and peed myself, and something about a shuttle launching from Freeport. You got anything else?" Cassie asked.

"Nope. When you're awake, I'm awake. When you're out, I'm out too," Alethia said.

As Alethia spoke, it was customary she would talk and busy herself with straightening out her own satchel, adjusting her clothing, checking her fingernails, or fixing something. Alethia was in the middle of adjusting her new outfit, seeing her range of motion, and taking a peek to see that there was no other undergarment when Cassie asked the next question.

"And when I dream?" Cassie asked.

Alethia stopped what she was doing and looked at her.

"What? When you're dreaming? No. It's like when you're awake, and you have thoughts. I can't read your mind, and I can't see your dreams. What kind of superpowers do you think I have?" Alethia said.

Cassie gave a quick nod in hopes it would end the conversation.

"You're right, Alethia. Let's see what they left for us," Cassie said quickly.

Initially skeptical, Alethia moved on as well.

Cassie rummaged through her satchel to find everything she had brought with her was still in place. She took out her transceiver radio and put it in scan mode and went back to sorting out what was new.

"Good idea. Maybe we can catch some intel. Are you up to get moving, or want to get more rest?" Alethia asked.

"I'm done with resting. Let's see what they left me, in addition to the new clothes," Cassie said.

"How did they get your clothes clean?" Alethia said.

Cassie unfolded her compression top and bottom and found that somehow both were clean.

"I have no idea. Maybe they pooled water? I hope they didn't have to use much. They are too kind," Cassie said.

"Well, you did save their friends' lives, and you got them some of that squid juice too. Who knew that was a thing? How do you feel?" Alethia asked.

"Actually, very rested, come to think of it," Cassie said.

Cassie was looking at a new item, a sixteen-inch blowpipe, like the one her team had used to subdue

Bennett and his team years ago but larger, more ornate, and better carved. She looked at a small pouch that held about twelve darts that had some cloth on the tips avoid pricking oneself. The pouch unfurled, allowing quick, unencumbered access to the darts, a good option considering the potency of the liquid at the tip. She raised it to see if it might attach to her chest rig on her satchel for easy access. It looked promising.

"The stuff they use is way stronger than what the doctor put together, isn't it?" Alethia asked.

"My experience with this stuff is something I would never want to do again. Yeah, I think it's stronger stuff," Cassie said.

It seemed as if Alethia was going to respond when the transceiver broke into static. The scanner stopped at a potential frequency, and Cassie took a minute to dial in for better reception.

" . . . Repeat overwatch. Come again? Did you say you sent Patties packing, half assed and still half baked? Bad copy, WSIB-413. Repeat. KC1-WVS."

There was brief silence.

"Half assed and half baked?" Cassie repeated.

"I'm guessing, well, half dressed and out of their minds or something," Alethia speculating like Cassie.

"Good copy, KC1. Eight Patties made it to Freeport Twelve center; they were dropped with squid juice and were out of it for most of the night and this morning. We took their uniforms for material, ate their rations, which sucked, but left them with some water, embarrassed but alive. All true."

The radio operator sounded genuine and joyful in what he was saying.

Cassie was stunned. She looked at Alethia, and she looked shocked.

"No way," Alethia said.

"Good copy, WSIB. You guys know how to party. Why'd you let them go?"

Cassie immediately wondered the same thing, but the answer came fast. The response was no surprise. She knew Patrician arrogance, the servicemen's in particular, very well.

"If their embarrassment doesn't kill them, Mars will. They've been planet-side, like, two and a half sol days, and they can't even keep their clothes on. What's the word on the teams we missed? Copy, KC1?"

"Good copy—elements of Third Platoon found both scouting parties from earlier. All of them gave up as soon as they saw the opposing forces. They surrendered and kept their clothes."

"And that shuttle?"

"Elements of civilian militia group caught those two and brought them to Fort Deadly. It's just like the mayday said: one Pattie pilot and a plebe. They surrendered too. Wanted sanctuary. They got sanctuary. It worked out well for the plebe woman. Not sure about the guy. Word is he kept her alive and helped her escape. An act of kindness from a Pattie? Strange times. You copy?"

"Good copy, KC1. Strange times indeed. Catch you next shift. Offset fifty megahertz. Stay frosty. WSIB-413, out."

"Good copy. KC1-WVS, out."

The transceiver fell back to static. The scan indicator blinked green, indicating it was hunting for more radio activity.

For the most part, Cassie was genuinely speechless. That was rare. She sat quietly. About fifty hours ago, maybe sixty, she'd heard that a large squad of motivated Patricians came down looking for her, and now four were captured, two surrendered, and eight more were running out of Freeport half naked with little to no resources. It was unclear if Alethia was just giving her space or just giving her time to come to a logical decision.

"So, I'll just mention this once, and I won't say anything again," Alethia said.

It wasn't space her AI was giving her to process things, but a nice way of saying, "Go home and call it a day."

"Go ahead, Alethia."

"I think we should head back, reacquire Hall, and ask her to come along for an adventure, and never look back," she said.

Cassie thought it over. Alethia wasn't wrong. Truth be told, she never was. She started out with a plan to find and kill all those who were hunting her. Just over two Martian days later, that hunting party had deteriorated into a sad, small group of desperate men who bit off way more than they could handle.

Still, as logical as her AI was, Cassie was human. Not a stupid human, but someone who wanted closure.

"Let me give you a counter proposal," Cassie said.

"This should be good," Alethia said.

"I will track these idiots down and make sure they are captured by the others. I won't engage. I won't go on a rampage or killing spree. I'll just go and watch it all unravel. How about that?" Cassie said.

Alethia stood still for a moment with her arms crossed. It was if she was thinking and had an option to disagree and take control of Cassie's body to go elsewhere.

"Perfect. You save face, I remain correct, and no one gets hurt. All winners, if you ask me," Alethia said.

"All true," Cassie said.

After a moment of pulling her thoughts together, Cassie found herself looking down and then around. It was obvious that Alethia was aware that something was going on.

"What's wrong?" she asked.

"You know, I might not be going anywhere for a while. I'm pretty high up, and I can't afford to injure myself," Cassie said.

"Hmm, I wonder if that was another reason Sarah and everyone else put you up here. Slow you down? Let nature take its course? Let Mars eat them up? They really do know you well, or at least, they're a good judge of character. To know you is to spend time with you," Alethia said.

Cassie wondered if it was a joke or if Alethia had a point.

"You know, I think you're right," Cassie said.

Cassie thought about the last part of what Alethia had said: to know someone is to spend time with them. Alethia had been in her head for years, but there was a lot she did not know about her. She might have been an AI, but she was based on someone who was carbon-based and had a past in a bygone world that was real, that formed the basis of her silicon-based existence.

I wonder if she knows herself, Cassie thought.

13

·–··

LEE FELT both exhausted and totally rested at the same time. He had a clear memory of moving deep into Freeport, came to a town square by the looks of it, and then his men started dropping like flies. He remembered being the last one standing and watching at least two of his men running away before they went down, then feeling two or three pricks at his neck and exposed hand.

After darkness, he had a running experience of being totally still, then moving, jolting at times, then back to stillness. There were times when he felt he was close to waking up. He would slowly emerge from a deep sleep and see blurred visions at first that changed into people, men and women of all colors, all scantily dressed and in various positions of movement.

Dancing, he thought.

Once the images came and faded, the darkness would fill with loud noise, rhythmic sounds with beats. Then he was awake again, still unable to move and see more movement, like before. And then he would fade again.

Music? Dancing? What the fuck are these savages doing? he thought.

Immobilized, still floating in and out of consciousness, Lee was convinced he and his men were at the center of a massive party. The more he saw, the more evident it became. Dim and dark at times, he had clear views of legs and torsos moving, dancing, and at times simply standing around him as if he were a piece of furniture. Sometimes faces would come into view to check on him. To see if he was awake, they would say something, but the music blotted out what they said. They were all young people who held them captive; they were all civilians, men and women, not a uniformed soldier, hostile or otherwise, in sight. He saw them laugh and smile, clearly talking, drinking, and enjoying their time while he sat immobile, periodically catching glimpses of some of his men, all in a similar states of being propped up and not moving. When he fell back into darkness, it was a respite. When he awoke, he was terrified, fearing that these half-dressed, fool colonists would dare torture or kill him and his men.

Assholes! This is how they treat their prisoners! Paralyze them, mock them, and then kill them, he thought.

Lee felt both indignant and annoyed. He was angry his men missed the trap they were walking into, that they were now captured and would probably die due to their incompetence at the hands of mixed-breed, dimwitted colonists and their lower-breed allies.

This was the only way they could have gotten me. Not in a stand-up fight. Fuck them!

After each bout of anger and fury, he felt exhausted and would slip off into darkness again. Each time he awoke, sometimes jostled awake as if he were being moved, sometimes just on his own, he still experienced the madness of coming in and out of consciousness, not being able to stay grounded, at the mercy of music, mirth, and merriment.

At one point, he awoke and found he was propped up in a different position, closer to a bonfire than he would like.

His eyes darted left and right, and he could see his XO and Lyman across from him, naked, immobile, and looking terrified.

Lee felt angry and embarrassed. He was furious that this was how he was going to die. Not dignified as he should have been. Not in the captain's seat of his ship, but on a filthy, dusty planet by a bunch of savages. He felt himself slipping again, and he was hoping he would never wake up again.

Darkness fell. Finally, it was quiet. No sound, just heat. Lee wondered if he had already been burned alive and was finally leaving this shithole of a planet.

He coughed. It was the first involuntary movement that he had felt, the first experience of having agency over his body. He coughed again and opened his eyes. As the world became brighter in the perpetual twilight of Mars, he could see that he was lying on his side, facing one of his crewmen, Eben, who was beginning to stir.

Lee heard more coughing and then words, obviously someone talking, though he could not make out what they were saying. He could now feel the ground he was lying on. He felt a disconcerting pain forming in his right foot. He was glad to see he could fold and look in the direction of his feet. The sight was horrible. His right foot was covered with what looked like an arm-size worm; a childhood image he remembered of an ancient bug called a centipede came to mind. He could see it wrapping around his foot and ankle, with its legs or feet moving in unison. While he could now move, he was sluggish. The guttural yell that came from him was deep, strong, and surprising. This was the first time he had screamed in his life.

The massive worm on his foot either heard or felt the scream, stopped, and then immediately let him go and scurried off. He looked at his foot to see that it was red as if the epidermis had been peeled away, and it hurt like hell.

"What the fuck," was all Lee could say. He said it a couple of times. He only stopped when he was pulled up by strong arms, then moved backward and placed in a chair.

"I got you, sir! You're okay. We got you," Henson said.

Lyman was already looking at Lee's foot. While grateful, Lee was distracted by both the shooting pain and the fact that his cook, XO, and other men he could see were still naked. For some reason, Lee thought he was going to be burned alive, and that's why he and his men were undressed. He found he was confused to be alive but still without clothes. For some reason, not having clothes bothered him greatly.

Lee looked around the immediate area. Some men moved around slowly, obviously looking for their uniforms and kit, while Henson and Lyman were focused on duty. Lee found that the low light in the underground world was dark as usual, but his eyes still hurt. As his hearing cleared, he wondered if something was wrong with his nose. He couldn't escape the smell of urine and feces.

"Report," Lee said.

He watched his XO's jaw slacken at first, then look down at Lyman, who stopped investigating Lee's foot and then went back to it as his XO appeared to pull himself together.

"Henson, you're the XO. What's going on?" Lee said.

"Well, sir, from what little I can ascertain, we were ambushed, rendered immobilized, and left to die on this hellhole," Henson said.

"If they wanted us dead, we'd be dead. We walked right into a kill box, and instead of wasting us, they darted us down like dogs, stripped us, had a party, and left us ass-naked and alive to live in shame," Lyman said.

Lee looked at Lyman, who had an expression that was a combination of annoyed, pissed, and embarrassed.

"I'm going to look for some clothes and kit," the cook said, then walked away without being dismissed. On his backside, Lee saw there was dark matter pressed on the cook's buttocks and upper thighs. Lee looked down, opened his thighs, and saw that he too had dried feces stuck to his skin.

"Fuck me," Lee said.

"Sorry about the cook, sir. I guess we're all a little tapped out," Henson said.

Lee raised his foot to take a look. It hurt as if burned, and puss was now surfacing, but it wasn't as painful as it looked. Henson dropped to look at it as well, and after inspection, he looked at Lee, as if to give a diagnosis and prognosis.

"I think we'll have to cover it, and you'll need some support to get around, sir," he said.

Lee was annoyed at the obvious assessment.

"Sir, it looks like you were the farthest from the fire, which might have been the reason that thing got to your foot," Henson said.

Lee looked beyond him and could see that the fire, though low, was still there, throwing off heat.

"I'm the only one that thing latched on to," Lee said.

"Yes, sir. I don't know about you, sir, but I swore we were going to be burned alive," Henson said.

"It might have been better, XO. This is bullshit," Lee blurted out.

Henson's demeanor went from calm to quiet.

"Yes, sir. Your orders, sir," Henson said.

Finally, some semblance of honor and dignity, Lee thought.

"Spread out in pairs in a grid pattern, and locate our uniforms, weapons, and kit. Pull the men together, and prep them for immediate fallback to our original position," Lee said.

"Yes, sir. Immediate fallback to our arrival site, sir? Regroup?" Henson said.

"Yes. Regroup, link up with our scouts, and find our

shuttle. We have a job to do, and we've been wasting time," Lee said.

Lee had been looking at his foot. When he hadn't heard an acknowledgement of his order, he looked up. By the time he locked eyes with his XO, Henson had confirmed the order.

"Yes, sir: Refit, fall back, regroup, and prep for mission. I got it, sir," Henson said.

"Good," Lee said.

Lee watched Henson move on. Like him, he was covered with dirt, dust, and darker matter that was probably dried fecal remnants. Lee went back to looking at his injured foot, wondering how he was going to effectively march back without full use. He touched it, and it was sore, though it looked far worse than it felt. Annoyed at his condition and the lack of enthusiasm from his XO and men, Lee started a reassessment of his recommendations for his team once they completed their mission.

We've got to get this mission back on track, Lee thought.

14

—··

BENNETT WATCHED Sherman take point ahead of him with Cadets Jefferson and Knowles on the flanks. They were armed with old-fashioned automatic rifles and sidearms, all with redundant field rations, radio rigs, edged weapons, ammunition, and essentials for a three-day search-and-recovery mission. Bennett felt like a civilian contractor or VIP as he walked along in light Fort Deadly red camo battlefield dress with just a sidearm, water, and rations. His team's kit seemed overkill for a one-klick walk to meet Captain Taylor's shuttle group, but it was obvious the landing was a launch point for a mission. While there had been radio silence from the *Lee,* the cryptic message giving coordinates and time, sent out in old international Morse Code, was more than enough for him to figure out support from above to recapture the mutineers was on the way.

"Now, Cadets, stay alert, and don't gawk at the task force when they land. They might be older, well armed, and have more toys, but they have limited knowledge and exposure of the land. If we break into teams, don't be surprised if you're put on scout recon," Sherman said.

"What? Whoa, I'm just . . ."

Sherman cut Jefferson off before she could finish.

"You're a *Fort Deadly* cadet, military trained and born and bred to survive in this hell. Most of the men have never been planet-side; they haven't left the air-conditioned, self-contained world of comforts like soft beds, prepared food, easy access to water, and medicine. The only thing they did right was cut their hair, change their uniforms, and have weapons and kit that suit this planet, but they are not experienced in living here, like you and Knowles. It will take them at least a week to acclimate. Do not underestimate and undersell yourself. You get me, Cadets?"

"Yes, sir," Jefferson and Knowles said.

The team moved ahead to the landing coordinates, painfully aware of every smell, sound, and sight in their immediate surroundings. With little warning, Bennett found himself already at the edge of a tall, crowded ring of boulders, short gray-green shrubs and man-size mushroom-like vegetation meeting an empty space of flat, red dust and dirt perfectly sized to accommodate two of the *Lee's* shuttles side by side if necessary. In the distance, Bennett heard the subdued roar of approaching shuttles. Before the roar grew, he waved his two cadets closer to talk to them both.

"Chief Sherman is right—you have the tactical and home field advantage here. Any officer who sees that will ask you to lead, not follow. If you are asked or ordered, do not hesitate, do not counter, and do not doubt—if these men are anything like I used to be before I got here, they will be disoriented, physically challenged by the environment, and poised to make mistakes either due to arrogance or ignorance. Under Captain Taylor's command, it will likely be out of lack of experience that they will mess up and not out of being an asshole. Trust yourself. You understand?" Bennett said.

"Yes, sir," the cadets said.

"Good. Eyes everywhere. Anything that looks out of

place, say something, and remember, this is your planet—they're all friendly visitors in a hostile land."

"Understood, sir," Knowles said.

"Crystal clear, sir," Jefferson said.

Bennett looked ahead to Sherman, who gave him the thumbs-up and then pointed overhead behind them. Bennett caught the bottom of a small shuttle, maybe a three- or four-man vehicle, as it suddenly decelerated, then banked hard starboard. After one complete turn to survey the area, it slowed even more but remained high above to allow for two other shuttles to come into its airspace.

As one of the larger crafts descended, the second one joined the fighter shuttle in overwatch.

"Let's move," Sherman said.

Without hesitation, Sherman approached the landing site of the first shuttle just as it landed, dropping both starboard and port ramps and bay doors, releasing two squads each side. Their dispersal was clean, well spaced, and covered all lines of fire. The first man who touched ground did not wait for the others to deploy but came out immediately to meet with Bennett and his team. Like the men who secured the area, he wore BDU strikingly familiar to what he and Fort Deadly's forces were wearing, though a darker, tan-brown color, and tactically armed and outfitted similarly as well. Bennett was surprised to see that Captain Taylor had not only "gone native" on field BDU, foot gear, and supplies, but the energy-based laser rifles and sidearms were all absent, replaced by gunpowder firearms clearly traded, reclaimed, and repurposed for planet-side operation.

"Captain Taylor's been busy with the refit," Bennett yelled out to Sherman over the now-ascending shuttle.

"He takes the mission of MAC–SOG seriously and has used every bit of intelligence he has," Sherman yelled back.

Bennett nodded and looked beyond him at the approaching officer. He then took a quick look at the cadets.

He was pleased to see them focused on the corners and edges of the field, potential points of danger and live fire if shit were to go sideways. They were all business and not the typical teens he remembered from decades ago on Earth.

But then, what is a typical adolescent on Mars where there are three-headed dog monsters, cats the size of transports, and daily weather that makes hell look like a day at the beach? he thought.

It took a moment, but then the familiar face finally made its way to his memory and was confirmed by Sherman.

"Lieutenant Evans! What is a starship navigator doing on a search-and-recovery mission in this hellhole?" Sherman said.

The positive energy of respect and friendship could not be understated. Unable to salute, and not in an environment for friends to hug, their exchange still exuded warmness that Bennett readily recalled from the first time and last time he'd met Evans on Captain Taylor's ship.

"Just me trying to get a break from the excitement of our mutineers and the damage they left behind," Evans said.

Bennett smiled at the exchange, and he saw Evens look at him and wink.

Bennett smiled again, chuckled even, trying to remember the last time a soldier at least three decades younger than him actually winked.

"Nice to see you, Captain Bennett!" Evans yelled out over the sound of the second transport shuttle landing.

"Glad to be alive and be seen, Lieutenant," Bennett said.

Bennett looked beyond the men and listened, watching two sets of squads take the place of the previous group, who in turn, moved into the edges of cover to secure even more of the landing site. As the men spoke, Bennett saw a man outfitted with tools and cases and a woman, uniformed and armed like the soldiers who walked with just the shade of a limp.

"Captain Taylor needs you back on the *Lee* to lead

repairs. He sent Second Engineer Ellis to take your place here and to see if the stolen shuttle can be at least rehabbed for in-atmosphere use," Evans explained.

"Are you saying the captain missed me?" Sherman said.

"Yes, sir. Ellis did a great job covering, but the *Lee* needs its chief engineer, and the captain owes Commander Strong a good engineer," Evans said.

Bennett squinted his eyes and looked just behind the arriving engineer. The woman's gaze was everywhere, searching for a threat or where a possible shooting platform or fire point could be.

"We picked up Specialist Hall's comm on the way and gave her a lift. Her skills will be well suited for our needs," Evans said.

Bennett felt his lips curl at the end and did his best to keep from a full-blown smile. It had been more than two months since she had gone deep into the mountains and lava flats to pick up Kurtz's trail, and it would be safe to say he missed her company, just as a father might miss a favorite daughter. As Bennett was married to his career and had no family, Betsy Ann Hall and Virgil Johnson were as close to family as he would ever have, even if they were like adult children from a first marriage that ended on good terms.

The shuttle engine's whine dropped but remained idle, allowing for conversation to drop below yelling but still talking loudly.

Sherman turned to Bennett and the cadet.

"Well, Bennett, it was nice working with you again. Keep an eye on my engineer and keep him focused. Not everyone can be as laser-honed and brilliant as myself," he said.

"Will do. Pleasure was mine, and I hope to see you soon, Chief. Stay safe," Bennett said.

Sherman nodded and addressed the cadets.

"Stay focused and frosty—you young cadets know this planet. Own it," Sherman said.

Both cadets made eye contact, nodded, and went back to scanning.

Before anything more could be said, the moment of awkwardness, sadness, and poignant goodbye was gone as Sherman trotted to the waiting shuttle, high-fiving his replacement.

Just then, Bennett heard one of his cadet's radios come to life with a transmission. Knowles moved off to pick up the comms. Similarly, Lieutenant Evans's comms did the same thing. He turned to listen in. This left Bennett to address Ellis and Hall.

"First time planet-side, Ellis?" Bennett said.

"Fourth time, sir. Salvage operations on all the abandoned outposts last year, Freeport Nine and Seven, and refit for water purification at Freeport Twelve. I hate to be that guy, but I like the heat and the work," he said.

Bennett smiled at the response and then focused on Hall.

"It's been too long. How have you been?" he asked.

"You know us plebes, Captain. We love the oppressive heat, hostile environment, and impossible missions," Hall said.

To the ear unfamiliar with their relationship, this response would have been merely factual. Coming from Hall, it was an expression of familiarity and closeness. The class and social distance between Patrician and plebe, while better than those between a slave and such, was very distant, not allowing for anyone below a Patrician to instigate and engage in a conversation, let alone start one with such familiarity.

Bennett smiled. He caught a curious look from Cadet Jefferson and decided to give a synopsis of their new team.

"Second Engineer Ralph Ellis, under the command of Lieutenant Commander W. T. Sherman of the heavy navy cruiser *Robert E. Lee,* and Specialist Betsy Ann Hall, attached to Military Assistance Command–Studies and Observation

Group, reestablished by Captain Taylor and his command team for the entire expedition force and Mars mission. Hall formerly trained and served in OPCST—Off-Planet Colonial Survival Training. Specially trained, varied experience, and well-known quantities. Their skill sets will be valuable to say the least," Bennett said.

The shuttle whine of the engine intensified, and the dust began to swirl again as the ship ascended with his colleague and friend heading back to work on the *Lee*. Just as the ship was moving out of airspace, the remaining ships kept circling at alternating orbits for overwatch. It had been years since Bennett, a former captain himself, had seen such excellent symmetry and military operation, air and field.

Bennett felt a presence beside him. It was Knowles. His look was well maintained as neutral, an excellent quality for very young soldiers.

"Sir, Field Officer Johnson and Third Platoon report capturing half of the mutineers except for their XO and a few others," Knowles said.

Bennett felt his eyes widen and a feeling of shock that he was sure he did not hide well. He looked back at his cadet, who nodded that was what he'd heard.

"Confirmed, Cadet. Our comms picked up chatter from local radio observers and a brief confirmation from Third Platoon: All but Robert Lee and the remaining half have surrendered and are detained by ground forces. You didn't leave much work for us to do here, sir," Lieutenant Evans said.

Bennett nodded and stood still for a moment. He was trying to figure out how an audacious plan to mutiny could fall apart so fast. He wondered if it had been a haphazard plan, something thrown together at the last moment, but then based on Glenn's interrogation, this had been months, maybe more than a year in the works. He wondered if there was internal strife, a rift in the mutineers' ranks once they landed, but then, one would have expected loyalty of some kind since they were all looking at the gallows together if they did coalesce as a group fast.

"Sir?" Knowles said, clearly worried if another fainting spell was pending.

Bennett waved his concern off.

"I'm good, Cadet. I'm just trying to figure out how this whole thing, this mutiny and their mission to capture Kurtz, all fell apart at lightning speed," Bennett said.

With the exception of shuttles flying above their heads, there was little background noise other than the ambient cavern sound.

"Well, the XO and Henson were big on talk but not on deed, or that's at least what the chief would say," Ellis said.

Bennett smiled at the statement. The first time he'd met Ellis was after seeing Lee exiting the chief's engine room with a bloody nose. Ellis had been willing to take the fall for Sherman's response to Lee's bullying.

"You're being kind, Ellis. The XO thinks he is he's entitled to a ship, leadership, and respect without the corresponding duty, discipline, work, and honor," Evans said.

"I know, but their whole operation lasted three days," Bennett said.

"Seventy-eight hours and thirty minutes plus," Evans corrected.

Wow. That's it? Bennett thought.

"Wait a minute: You're Virgil's friend? Navigator on the *Lee*? How come you're leading the task force?" Hall asked.

Hall jogged Bennett's memory of the first time he'd met Virgil; he had made a mistake and frozen, and Evans stepped in to help and not undercut his authority, hard to do as officers on a ship.

"Change of pace. Been here a couple of times and like the ambience. Thought I'd stop by to see how my old friend was doing and bring justice to mutineers that hurt my ship. No real reason," Evans said with a smile.

A series of dots and dashes erupted from Evans's transceiver mike latched to his chest plate. All were silent to hear and decipher the message. Bennett thought he was hearing more numbers, then determined it was that and more. Hall was the first to talk.

"Solid coordinates—just outside Freeport's exterior wall. We're about four hours by foot, twenty minutes by flight," she said.

Before Hall even finished her sentence, Evans was already on the move. He made a circle motion to huddle up, and noncommissioned officers ran up. Evans was quick to set a plan in motion.

"I'll be taking Bravo, Charlie, and Juliet squads to the coordinates. Charlie and Juliet with support of Third Platoon will manage the prisoners while I'll take Bravo and the Fort Deadly team to find the XO inside Freeport. I want you to secure this landing site to receive and secure prisoners when I get back; process and bring them back to the ship. Make sure there is a solid defensive perimeter with trips to keep runners in and the curious out," Evans said.

After a minute, he turned to ask Bennett a question.

"Sir? I would like to deploy your team in the following way—Specialist Hall and your cadets would be useful in tracking and finding Lee in Freeport. I would ask if you could be the field officer to coordinate this location with elements of Fort Strong for additional security and resources, and I'd like to send Second Engineer Ellis with Fire Team Zeta to deal with the shuttle. Thoughts?" Evans asked.

Bennett took a moment to review the plan. It made logical sense. He was the obvious choice to be left behind to make sure supplies and security were established between Fort Deadly and this base camp, and smart to have the younger, native elements of his team be part of the hunting party.

"No complaints here. Good hunting, and I'll see you when you get back," Bennett said.

Evans nodded, and with rapid motion of his hands, he sent his teams into motion. He waved the shuttle to come down for pickup and was already giving orders on comms for the next step.

Bennett deliberately looked at both cadets, did not engage their expressions of disbelief, and pointed at them to follow the lieutenant to the descending shuttle.

"Remember what I said: Stay alert, keep focus, trust your instincts, and watch you six," he said.

"Yes, sir," they both said in unison, and moved as directed.

Bennett looked after them, his expression melting from calm and collected commanding officer to worried grandparent watching his loved ones head into danger. Hall, watching the whole interchange, smiled and drew close.

Even though she had been in the field for months, she nonetheless looked rested and fit for combat. How she managed to secure an updated ship uniform and kit modified for the underground world from the *Lee* was a marvel, though not totally unexpected coming from Captain Taylor.

"I got them covered. They'll be fine," Hall reassured.

"Thank you," Bennett said.

Not wanting to seem like the old relic veteran of foreign wars looking on as his kid and grandkids went off to war, he turned to find focus. It didn't take him long.

"Sir, permission to leave camp with Fire Team Zeta to salvage the shuttle," he heard Ellis say.

Oh yeah. I'm in charge of something, Bennett thought.

"Yes. Go," Bennett said.

Before he could reconsider his order and ask for

timelines, the men were off, and another young soldier came up with a question.

"Sir, the men were asking where we should set the latrines, where you want overwatch, and any hazards we should know before we deploy," the young man asked.

Behind him, Bennett saw another pair of soldiers coming up. One was obviously overheated and sick, and the other was carrying a transceiver for comms.

It had been a while since Bennett had been in actual field command. He felt grateful. He could never have guessed or imagined he would be where he was right now—a former disgraced officer, close to sixty years old, in good health, living a great life as an Earth transplant to a hotter-than-hell underground world on Mars with no life-extending medical benefits.

This is great, he thought.

15

"HONESTLY, I feel bad for him. I mean, look at him," Alethia said.

Cassie sat back down below the small wall from her perch to take a moment to fully process all the data spinning around in her head. She nodded to herself and then went back to her overwatch position just to confirm her sightings, even though she knew they were still happening in real time.

Overhead, the subdued but clear roar of approaching and receding shuttle craft engines added to the need to limit exposure to the sky, so when she found a four-story building, the limit for Freeport residential construction that had a decorative overhang for a sun that never came out—with wind chimes, no less—it was the perfect place to spy on her target and scurry and hide when and if shuttles came by for a recon.

Cassie peered through her scope right in front of her location, looking again at the field that sat between Freeport's outer building and a crumbled perimeter wall. She watched a flurry of activity with soldiers, mostly men in uniforms armed with firearms clearly holding sentry points in well-organized groups of three by that broken wall, with a single-file line of naked men with hands atop their head, clearly prisoners, flanked by still more armed men. She did a mental count in her head on just how Lee's group disintegrated – two pairs of scouts were captured by Third Platoon, a pilot and woman captured and asked for asylum, and now this group, presumably the last of her target's group, were now surrendering.

"How the mighty have fallen. With these seven caught, in addition to the others yesterday, that makes thirteen in total. Twelve if you subtract the woman they originally kidnapped," Alethia said.

"Naked and weak. Embarrassing," Cassie said.

"That means that guy is probably the last one, and I bet he's the brains of this whole operation, if you could call it an operation," Alethia commented.

"Yup. Alone and demoralized and injured. This is too easy," Cassie said, though her tone and expression were distant as if she were deep in thought elsewhere. She was.

While normally, she might have found the naked men to be the anomaly, the soldiers and their uniforms held her focus as well as the command group. The earlier transmission she'd tapped into warned her about the naked men and their condition, but seeing the two types of soldiers was still surprising.

It was easy to identify two of the three sets of uniforms, as she had seen them often on the planet: One clearly came from Fort Deadly, under the command of Virgil Johnson, and the other was from the civilian militia out of Freeport. It was the third set of uniforms, similar BDUs with differing color, though not bad for Mars's environment, that drew her attention. Closer observations identified just how different these soldiers were from the others. These soldiers were clearly better fed, with full heads of hair, not as lean and clearly not adapted to Mars based on their sluggish, unsteady, laborious gaits, and persistent wiping of their faces.

"They must be from the *Lee*. Well equipped and fed but not used to the place at all," Cassie said.

"That Captain Taylor is a pretty savvy guy. You think he copied some of the strategies and tactics from Fort Deadly?" Alethia said.

"No doubt. He got everything right, but the men will need a lot more time to adjust," Cassie said.

"If it's true the mutineers left in a hurry, they probably didn't have the same preparations these guys do," Alethia said.

It was easy to imagine the arrogance and miscalculations Patrician military men could make, especially officers. She had been shocked when she'd come face-to-face with Bennett years after his command. He'd looked frail, small, but that was nothing to how much he had changed from when he'd commanded his own ship. His focus to save his crew at his expense, to save a lowly Patrician officer and a mixed-heritage woman was baffling, incomprehensible, at the time. And then, their genuine loyalty to him was nothing short of stunning. That was unique.

Cassie focused her attention on Virgil and a similar-looking soldier dressed like he'd come from the *Lee*. Farther away from them, closer to the middle of the field far away from the columns of men, she recognized Specialist Hall, dressed in the same BDUs as the visitors, along with two strikingly younger soldiers, maybe cadets, a boy and girl, dressed in Fort Deadly BDUs, clearly scanning possible snipper and overwatch positions. She dropped again as the girl's scanning came into her field of vision.

"And it really is Hall," Alethia said.

"Sure is. She's not wearing Fort Deadly or a militia uniform but the *Lee*'s uniform," Cassie said.

Cassie couldn't help but feel a heavy weight in her

stomach and heart at the thought of Hall returning to the *Lee*. She was struggling with why she would be wearing an off-world uniform when she typically sported one better suited for her work in the field. Cassie continued to look down and then refocused her attention back to her own mission. The silence clearly conveyed something to her AI implant.

"You know, there may be another reason for her wearing that uniform. I mean, she was obviously picked up and transported here. She's good at survival and tracking, but there is no way she could have made it here like we did with her prosthetic leg, and she more likely went the long way to avoid, well, some of the things we had to deal with," Alethia offered as possible reasons.

Cassie was back up scanning the tops of the settlements a couple of rows in and saw her target again. The man was pale, his face contorted in an array of emotions, his fist hitting the small wall as his other hand violently lifted and put down a set of binoculars. Too far away to hear, she was sure he was swearing and pissed off. It was clear he was naked and struggled to stay steady on his feet. He was half standing and kneeling and leaning against a wall that gave him much-needed support and a prime view of the activity in the field. She cocked her head to assess where the shuttles might be relative to her position and was pleased to hear more receding than approaching engines.

"Well, if I'm having a bad day, this guy is having a profoundly worse day," Cassie muttered.

Cassie continued watching and then zeroed in on his location by noting the surrounding building's features, numbers, and distance. While Freeport and other former colonial outposts seemed to be identical, each had unique physical features and layouts that made it possible to identify and navigate locations. Built by nanobots, all residential buildings had three or four stories, a common landing per floor with three rooms at the top while the stairs continued up. This section of Freeport appeared to have long been emptied, with nothing left behind.

"He sure is having a bad one," Alethia said.

Cassie prepared to leave her position to confront the man who allegedly was hunting her down. It was amazing how things could change in three sol days. Out of habit, she looked back to the field and saw that the prisoners were long gone but Virgil, the other soldier, and elements of Fort Deadly, the *Lee*, and the militia were still in place. Hall and the other team were gone. Cassie made wider sweeps her scope, but she found no trace of them. She packed up everything and made for a quick exit.

"Well, that's interesting. Hall and the two kids are gone," she said.

By now, Cassie was on the move, heading down the stairs with an internal map in her head where she was going but totally no idea what she was going to do when she was face-to-face with the man.

Still wearing her recently gifted Freeport long skirt and halter top, she was pleased by how it moved with ease and no noise—not that her compressed clothes did, but the flow of her movements was graceful and silent. With her satchel in front and pack on her back, she kept her hands free in case she needed both for defense, offense, or something unexpected.

"If those two kids are with Hall and armed as she is, I'd say they are cadets native to Freeport, and they are already looking for our guy. Maybe we should just let them do the work and watch them take him. I mean, the guy is hopeless, not worth our time and effort," Alethia said.

Cassie pressed on in silence. She knew that Alethia was right. What started out as a heated plan to end a threat geared to ending her life again had devolved into an injured and naked officer who watched his men abandon him. Honestly, even if she did kill him, the situation and circumstance would be that of a human squashing a bug and being happy about it.

As she moved in silence, she prepared her blowpipe with a squid dart and carefully made haste without noise. It didn't take her long to hear a man's voice, clearly angry and complaining. The shuttle engines still seemed far off, but she was shocked by the lapse of security and sound. He definitely was not in his right mind. She was clearly at the right location, and the man's presence was an unmistakable pinpoint—one floor up, second floor, close to an open window.

"This is embarrassingly easy, Cassie. Just dart the guy, send up a flare, and let's head to the Promised Land," Alethia said.

Cassie could tell Alethia was appealing to her sense of honor for herself and not compassion for a pitiful Earther, totally out of his element. Her AI had come to know her so well.

Cassie quietly ascended the stairwell and moved quickly, though the noise the man was making clearly obscured her approach. Once at the landing, she saw three doors. She was thinking about taking the left one first when she saw the man move slowly from the front door wall and back to the window, clutching a makeshift crutch, binoculars, and a laser rifle slung on his back. He was so laser-focused on getting to the window that he missed her presence. It took one second to sneak up behind him and shadow him to the window. He was unaware that if she wanted, she could have stabbed him repeatedly.

Cassie stopped right before he got to the window, his back turned and still not aware of her presence.

"Motherfuckers! If they think they can take me, they're far more stupid than I thought," the man said, furious and delusional based on the reality of the situation and his threats.

Cassie waited for the right moment to strike. He was positioned right in front of the window, half standing and still cursing. He had put the binoculars on the sill and leaned his crutch on the other side of the window, and he was working the tattered sash that barely kept his rifle in place to pull into offense position.

"Hey!" Cassie yelled from behind.

The man, totally startled, whipped around and moved backward as quick as he could. Since his back foot was clearly injured, he stumbled to the window. Momentum took hold, and he nearly catapulted out of the window, the back of his thighs and torso hanging out of the second-floor opening. His two arms shooting out and grabbing the window's side frame kept from falling. His expression was a combination of shock, fury, and surprise.

"What the fuck!" he shouted.

Cassie watched him hang precariously out the second-floor window, about thirteen to fifteen feet high, a survivable fall in most cases. A naked man, all tensed, falling backward onto a dusty or dirt surface was not great, but it was possible to live another day, she thought.

"Relax," Cassie said, then blew a dart from her blowpipe into his left pectoral. She watched him struggle to hang on while wanting to pull the dart out. She blew another one into his neck and watched him look down and then up at her, both confused and angry.

In less than five seconds, she watched him focus all his effort into his arms. He was slowly trying to pull himself in back through the window until the squid venom took hold. That's when his hands slackened, his eyes rolled back, and he fell quietly back out the window.

By the time she walked to see where he'd landed, he was splayed out on his back, arms and legs outstretched.

"Well, he might be alive. If the darts worked to relax all his muscles all at once, and he landed on his back with all limbs spread to absorb a fifteen-foot drop, he might be fine," Alethia said.

She waited to see if he moved. Instead, she caught movement from below to her left. She stepped quickly back out of view but close to the window. She heard one set of steps, quiet and light coming from the left and a similar set coming from the right.

"Shit! We've got company. Hall and friends," Alethia said.

"Yes," Cassie said softly.

Cassie stayed quiet. Listened intently. She was impressed by how Hall and her team had zeroed in on her location, though, to be fair, her target's noise level was that of a siren in a small cave. There was another set of steps that stopped along where she thought the body was lying right at the front of the entrance. Cassie knew that if they were there, the expected escape would be from the roof with a lot of running and jumping. The out-of-the-box, unexpected exit would be out the front door.

"Knowles—head to overwatch over there, fourth floor. Jefferson—call it in and get air support. He was dropped and still warm, so she may be close," she heard Hall say in a firm, hushed voice.

"Kurtz? No way," the boy said.

"Knowles—overwatch, now. Jefferson, call in coordinates now from over there," Hall said with no room for questions to follow.

Cassie heard a pair of feet run off in two different directions. As one moved slightly in front of the window, she heard the chirping of a transceiver picking up traffic.

Cassie bolted from the window and set the pair of binoculars and her blowpipe in the center of the floor. She moved back to the hall landing, went half a flight up, and waited. She was positive that Hall knew she might be around. Why else put on kid on overwatch and the other down the street to get help fast?

Cassie waited in silence. She was pleased that Alethia was aware enough not to make herself available. It took a long minute, but Hall's step, uneven and louder than she probably wanted due to her prosthetic leg, made its way upstairs to the second floor. The steps stopped suddenly, probably scanning and assessing the room in front of her that revealed binoculars and a blowpipe.

The steps started again, then sped up and went right, then quickly went left to clear the flanking rooms. Then she heard Hall rush the middle. Cassie moved close to the middle door, counted for five seconds to allow Hall to think all was clear, then rushed into the room.

Hall was on one knee, holding the binoculars in one hand and picking up the blowpipe with another when Cassie laid eyes on her. Hall's eyes first registered shock, then resolve as she dropped both items and reached for her rifle by her foot. Cassie unceremoniously tackled her, knocking her clear across the room. Before Hall could recover, Cassie slid in on top and behind her. She pulled Hall over in a sitting position with her legs crossed over her and her full arm across her throat, cutting off her air if need be. Hall's hands naturally went to her throat to loosen the hold, leaving her sides free for her crisscrossed legs to tightly squeeze.

"Shh, Hall. Stop moving, and I'll loosen up," Cassie said.

After a moment of struggling, testing the grip, Hall stopped and waited.

"Okay. Why are you looking for me?" Cassie asked.

"We are looking for the guy on the street," she said.

"No. You were looking for me at the lava flats klicks from the first mountain. Right when their shuttle blew in from the surface three days ago," Cassie said.

Hall's body first tightened and then seemed to relax.

"I thought I was being watched. It just didn't feel right," Hall said.

Cassie tightened her arm as Hall responded, then loosened it again.

"Focus, Hall. Why are you looking for me?" Cassie repeated.

"I wanted to know more about this Promised Land. Go see it. See if we all could go. Bennett suggested I look for you and ask rather than just go on a search and sweep," Hall said.

Cassie was quiet for a moment. The roar of shuttle engines approaching pulled her back.

"What are your intentions? Why go there?" Cassie said.

"Exploration. New science and . . . well, just to get away. Be free," Hall said.

Cassie's heart jumped, and her stomach felt light. But then, a wave of anger flashed, and she tightened her arm a little.

"Why are you wearing this uniform?" Cassie said.

"What? This? I got a ride to get here from the *Lee*'s shuttle and took a uniform and kit," Hall said.

"You're not part of the crew?"

"The crew? On the *Lee*? Are you kidding? Captain Taylor is great. He's saved my life more times than I can count, but I'm free, here. Why would I go back to the *Lee*?" Hall asked.

The response, tone, affect, and logic all made sense. Cassie felt embarrassed to have thought otherwise and knew she would get a ton of shit from Alethia.

Cassie turned her focus back to Hall. The shuttle engines were getting close. Even though they were still some distance away, Freeport's dust and dirt were kicked up. The closer they got, the more of a dirt screen they would kick up for her.

"Go back to the lava flats, where we saw the ship. I'll talk to you then," Cassie said.

Cassie squeezed Hall's sides tightly to distract her from releasing her arm from her throat. That freed up her hand to snatch a waiting squid dart laced on her chest satchel.

Cassie felt genuinely bad for using it on her, but she knew Hall would not just let her walk away.

"I'm sorry," Cassie said, as she depressed the dart into Hall's neck. Surprisingly, Hall did not react until she simply slumped between her legs.

Cassie carefully moved Hall on her side just to make sure choking didn't happen. She was up on her feet, dropped a dart in her blowpipe, and ran to the window just as the roar of engines seemed to come from behind the building.

Cassie saw the young woman looking up at the approaching ship, covering her eyes from the dust storm the engines kicked up. Still, she seemed to have caught sight of Cassie and was raising her weapon to fire. Cassie was faster and blew the dart with all her force to hit the girl fifteen feet down where she stood above the man's body. She watched the girl's hand fly to her face and cry out as if she was stung by an insect. She seemed to recover and went to point the rifle back at her, but Cassie didn't wait to see if she could put the trigger. She was already descending the short flight to where the kid and body were, planning to use another dart if the girl was still a threat. She ran out on the street, red dust and dirt creating cover, letting her easily jump over one body and passed the girl, who was amazingly still up on her knees but failing, her rifle already on the ground.

Still aware that Hall had an overwatch, she ran in the opposite direction of where she'd heard the overwatch person went, in the direction where field troops more likely would come. She cleared two buildings by going through them, getting farther away from the shuttle's presumed landing. She stopped cold and hid just under a windowsill as elements of Third Platoon quietly moved through the streets. If she had been on the street exposed, she would have been cut down. She waited until at least twelve troops moved on. Then another pair came up, stopped, and moved ahead.

Once it was quiet, she picked up the pace and went perpendicular to the field where she had first seen the troops until she came to the last house by the perimeter wall.

Throughout her engagement with her target, then Hall and her team, the evasion of Third Platoon and the trek to her extraction point, Alethia had been unusually silent. For a moment, Cassie feared something might have happened to her, as if that were remotely possible.

"You know, it might not be there. You used that tunnel two years ago. Someone could have found it and blocked it up," Alethia finally said.

"Be optimistic," Cassie said.

By now, Cassie was drenched due to movement and stress. Her clothes were still loose, and she was happy to know that her cardio and stealth skills were still solid.

"Are you kidding? I've been holding my breath for ten minutes. If I could pee and poop, I would be doing just that everywhere," Alethia said.

Cassie took her time to survey the area. She was ten meters from the town wall and hopefully the entrance to a tunnel that hadn't been discovered. Before she moved, she made sure her kit was all in place and positioned in such a way that if the escape hole and tunnel were still there, she wouldn't be hung up by her gear.

Cassie took a deep breath and then sprinted across open fields, ten meters, thirty plus feet, a totally unobstructed view for any who might be looking.

She made it to the hole, found the cover—a mix of tarps, dust and dirt—and a waiting hole that should drop five feet and then thirty meters straight out. Hopefully, that exit wasn't discovered too. Once cleared, she dived in, then reassembled her cover. It was important.

"You are one lucky, hot bitch. I mean, you are the coolest," Alethia said.

Cassie couldn't help but smile. She had been lucky. No doubt. She was feeling competent and victorious.

"It's a shame you don't have the same conviction and insight in reading people as you do in close-quarter combat, evasion, and escape, though. Lots of skills but issues with intuition," Alethia said.

Cassie slowed to understand what Alethia was saying.

"Wait a minute. What?" Cassie said.

She was genuinely wondering what her AI meant.

"I mean, didn't I tell you that Hall probably needed a lift to get here, got a new uniform and kit, and was probably not part of the *Lee* crew?" Alethia said.

Cassie dropped down to the ground, then squatted to crawl about one hundred feet away, hoping not to run into new occupants of the escape tunnel or waiting troops.

"You're going to gloat about this for a long time, aren't you?" Cassie said.

"Yes, I am. A very long time," Alethia said.

16

LEE FELT himself trying to wake up, startled to hear what sounded like a shuttle engine, far but strong. He shook his head as if it would wake him faster, clear his head, and readjusted himself on the floor, propped up by a wall in one of the buildings close to where their shuttle had crash-landed about three days ago. He thought it might be three days ago, maybe longer. He was glad to hear the shuttle. It meant his plan of returning to the original landing site was now his exfil.

Lee nodded to himself and saw that while his foot looked bad, it didn't sting as much as it had earlier when he was struggling to get this far, to one of the abandoned structures on the second floor, he remembered. Ascending the stairs, as few as they were, was difficult due to the terribly constructed, makeshift crutch from Henson and his crew. The crew, with no clothes, limited water and no rations, and absolutely nothing to scavenge, made the short trek and focus on mission terrible.

Still, he was here, hearing a shuttle and looking forward to using the repaired vehicle to either go to the other end of

Freeport Twelve to search for supplies or fly to another colony to search.

"Conroy!" Lee called out.

Before Henson left to reunite with the scouts that had searched for Glenn and the shuttle, he reported some signs of the shuttle that was close by. He'd said that he was going to leave Conroy at ground floor and Eben on overwatch on the roof, giving a clear line of sight to the landing field.

"Conroy? Status," Lee called out again.

More silence answered him except for the varying sound of a shuttle engine.

Lee cleared his throat and was going to call out again when he heard something off about the engine noise. There sounded like there were two. One seemed to approach while another, faint, seemed to recede.

"Two? Fuck," Lee said.

He immediately realized that if there was more than one shuttle, it might not be Glenn at all but shuttles from either the *Lee* or maybe a shuttle Fort Deadly borrowed from one of the larger colonies.

"No, no, no! Conroy, get up here. Find Eben! Find out what is going on," he said frantically.

As he yelled out orders, he struggled to get up off the floor without banging his foot, then to use his shitty crutch. He tried to keep his hastily made sling for his rifle from snapping in two, making it even more difficult to move around with limitations.

"Jesus Christ! Son of a bitch. Conroy? Where the fuck are you? Answer me!" he yelled.

Instead of calling to Conroy further, he prioritized getting a direct report from Eben, who was on overwatch. In his position, he should be able to identify location and number of the friend or foe shuttles in play.

Lee continued to curse under his breath, hobbling up one set of stairs, then another, until the doorless opening on the roof was right in front of him. He wanted to yell for Eben but figured out he could chew him and Conroy out later for not listening out for a superior officer's orders.

Finally, he was on the top floor and exiting the hall to the roof, where he was surprised to see that there was not a soul there. No Eben. No Conroy. No one. The only thing he saw was a set of binoculars set down on a small wall, maybe three feet tall to keep people from falling off the roof.

"What the fuck is this?" he snarled out.

Lee was so angry at the lack of security and the absence of his troops, he struggled with what to even say when he saw them next. It was only when he was halfway down for cover behind the wall when he saw two shuttles off in the distance circling in an overwatch search grid pattern that he wondered if he had been abandoned.

Not when *I see them next but* if *I see them next,* he thought suddenly.

He looked down at his foot again and readjusted his stance so he could take weight off it but not plop back onto the floor, below the wall. It was an off-balance position, but he used his arms to balance the binoculars to look over where the activity was happening.

Lee first scoped out the aerial situation. He identified two shuttles—one transport and another a fighter—both from the *Lee* and both in transport and suppressing fire position.

"No, no, no, no! This can't be happening," he said more as a growl than a cogent preference.

He dropped his field of vision first and located two familiar faces at the far end of the field, well armed and placed in solid fortified positions to cover all fields of fire. He immediately identified *Lee*'s navigator, Lieutenant Evans, and that mutinous dog who escaped justice with Bennett and the mixed-breed woman, Virgil Johnson, former helmsman. It was easy to see they were coordinating forces as the mix of *Lee*'s crew and Fort Deadly troops and local militia were all working together.

"No fucking way! This can't be possible," he said.

He moved farther back. Much to his surprise, he saw a column of men, naked, hands on top of their heads, walking single file, flanked by ground forces, all moving toward Evans and Johnson. They were all prisoners. All his men.

"No," he said quietly.

He zoomed in to see if he could identify who they were individually, but they all looked the same; naked, slow in gait with two unsteady on their feet, plodding along in a narrow, short line. A walk of shame.

Lee felt his chest tighten, the weight of an anvil sitting in his stomach, and his hands clutching the binoculars until his fingers hurt. He put the glasses down and slammed his fist on the short wall.

"Fucking, traitors! You motherfuckers! Henson! Lyman! I'll kill you all," he yelled out.

He dropped his head and tried to catch his breath.

"Fuck. Think, Lee. Think," he said, quieter than he had before. It was more whisper than a low voice.

Lee readjusted himself as best he could to keep from dropping on the floor to reestablish visual on his traitors and their defeat. As he scanned, he caught sight of a familiar woman. The one that had one leg, one of Taylor's pets who thought she was the shit in her uniform and MAC–SOG department. He narrowed the scope and saw she was now wearing one of Taylor's new BDUs, clearly working for him again. As he started a slow pullback, he saw another soldier, more a young boy, in a Fort Deadly uniform. As he pulled farther back, he caught sight of a young Black woman, also dressed in Fort Deadly BDU, looking right back at him through her rifle scope.

Lee's head snapped up from looking through the

binoculars, as if doing so would remove his image and location from her sight.

"Fuck," he said as he pulled himself up, then maneuvered as fast as he could to get off the roof. His first stop was the room where he'd woken up to see if there was anything—water, his sidearm, anything—that he could retrieve before exiting the structure and move in deeper into Freeport. He hoped the people there would dart anyone following him and thereby level the field.

He made it to the second floor with stumbling and looked where he had been sitting. Nothing was there. He was totally pissed at being physically hampered by his foot, naked with nearly nothing for resources. He moved to the window for a quick scan to see if the area was clear. As he hobbled to the window, he started reaching for his slung rifle, barely tethered to his back. He had a sudden image of being surrounded and needing to make a last stand.

"Motherfuckers! If they think they can take me, they're far more stupid than I thought," he said loudly.

Right when he was closing in on the open window, he heard a loud voice, a woman saying, "Hey!" right behind him, as if she were right on his ass.

Lee whipped around, turning faster than he had wanted, barely able to stand due to his foot. Because he was so startled, he backed up so quickly, he stumbled back and out of the window.

"What the fuck!" he shouted, totally caught off guard. He couldn't believe someone could get that close, inches from his back, without him knowing it at all.

If it weren't for his quick reflexes, rapidly outstretching his arms and hands to grip the window frames, he would have fallen right out. He hung on to the frame, stopping his backward momentum as his thighs, torso, and head all hung out the window with a drop of about fifteen feet below.

Lee tightened his grip, and for the first time, he was able

to shift focus to see who had yelled at him. It was indeed a woman, but he was confused whom she was for a moment. He had been looking for Cassandra Kurtz. Based on images gathered by old intelligence, he remembered her having pale skin, a uniform, short to shoulder-length hair, and a mildly athletic build. Looking at her longer, he recalled four or five images over the last year that were allegedly her, mostly shadowed by Mars's perpetual twilight, where she resembled the woman in front of him. She seemed smaller, compact, and he was surprised to see she wore a long dress and a revealing halter top, not exactly exuding insurrectionist and terrorist vibes.

It can't be her, he thought.

His thoughts raced to challenge that a woman—a civilian, really, with no military training—could sneak up on him without him knowing it. And yet, that's what happened. If such a feat was possible, maybe such a woman would be the infamous Kurtz.

His attention was grabbed by the woman saying, "Relax," which seemed more of a suggestion, not an order. The volume, tone, and cadence were low, firm with a natural rhyme. Without a second thought, she shot him with a dart from an ornate blowpipe right into his left breast.

What the fuck? Why? he thought.

He was still processing it, and he pulled as much as he could to get back inside when another dart hit him in the throat. He almost let go, but he focused on more strength to go to his grip and pull. He had a second when he thought he could make it, but just as before, he felt lightheaded, and his limbs were numb. Just when he felt like he was falling asleep, he had the sensation of flying, which felt very different from the first time he'd been hit with darts. A rapid sense of peace that came over him.

17

..---

BENNETT EMBRACED the calm joy of watching his young cadets, all circling around Cadet Jefferson's cot, hanging on every word about her mission that crossed paths with Cassandra Kurtz. Hall was recovering far slower than a thirteen-year-old girl might from a toxin. The report felt legitimate, with no fabrications and additions that might make the situation bigger than life. With Jefferson sitting up, talking with her hands, Knowles sat on the cot's edge, providing details from his perspective that supported and added to the narrative. All the while, nearly all fifteen of the cadet squads, except for Olson and Owen, who were monitoring comms, were enthralled. After the third request to "tell the story from the top," Bennett was no longer listening to the details, already documented in the cadets' after-action report, but enjoying the interaction, experiencing the camaraderie of the cadets' deepening bond, brothers and sisters in arms.

"I wish I could say it was a firefight, but she got the drop on me. By the time I got back from calling in reinforcements and looked up to the window, I had a dart buried in my face," Jefferson said.

"Did it knock you out immediately?" a cadet asked.

"Almost. I mean, I was able to get my rifle pointed in the general direction of the window, but I dropped to my knees and did a face-plant. But before that, as I was going down, I saw Kurtz bolt from the door, jump over me and that XO, and then it was darkness. I hoped Knowles here had a shot," she said.

On cue, the entire group's eyes leveled on Knowles, who by now was well rehearsed in his part of the story.

"I had nothing from overwatch. By the time the shuttles approached and zeroed in on our position, there was more dirt and debris flying, like Martian dirt devils you see aboveground. We all figured that if the guy fell from the second floor, and if Kurtz was still around, the best bet, fastest, most-direct exfil would be along the rooftops, but there was nothing," Knowles said.

"Whoa. And Specialist Hall?" another cadet asked.

Knowles nodded his head.

"She was hit with a dart too, though I heard the scene looked like a fight happened, and the dart that hit her was not there, as if she was stabbed with it rather than just hit," Jefferson filled in.

"That's speculation, Cadet," Bennett said, and moved toward the group surrounding the heroic teens. The group split to give way for him to approach the cot, all of them standing at attention, with Knowles jumping to his feet, and Jefferson moving as fast as she could to join them.

"As you were. Jefferson—don't you dare get out of bed," Bennett ordered.

"Yes, sir," she said, and she pulled her feet back to the cot to resume a prone position.

Bennett placed his hand on Knowles's shoulder and gave him a little push to sit back down.

"Cadet Jefferson's speculation may, indeed, be true, based on the condition and situation of the room they found her in. XO Lee and Jefferson had darts still in their body while Specialist Hall had an entrance wound but no dart. Why Kurtz would remove hers and not the others seems off. But once she recovers, we will find out if our theories are correct," he said.

"Maybe she didn't have time," one cadet offered.

"Maybe, Cadet. But if I know her, she has a nasty way of making things work, regardless of time and resources," he said.

Bennett was surprised how his tone was absent of emotion. For a person who'd lost his right eye and hand to a terrorist, his response was devoid of anger. It just seemed to be a fact.

Another cadet looked like she was going to ask more about Kurtz, but thankfully, the fort's chief medic, Sergeant Burns, interrupted.

"All right, Cadets. Let's give my patients and Captain Bennett a break. They need rest, and the captain needs to meet with Specialist Hall, who can talk a bit more easily now," he said.

Bennett smiled at both the save and the fact that Hall was in better shape than when he'd seen her earlier, sprawled out on a litter, totally out and messed up, and then semiawake but unresponsive nearly a full eight hours later.

"She's waiting for you, Captain," Burns said, and pointed him to the other end of the medical bay.

Bennett moved with all deliberate speed to see her and could still hear the cadets requesting to stay longer, wanting to hear more and be with their friends. Sergeant Burns, known for being a stickler for medical protocols and his patients' safety, was predictably insistent on their compliance to leave.

"Look, you mutant rug rats. Unless any of you are officers or hold a medical degree, or work for a living like us sergeants, get your shit together, say goodbye, and come back no sooner than 13:00 hours," he said loudly.

While he could hear the moaning and disappointment, he could tell the group was disbanding. By the time he got to Hall's cot, he was pleased that the chief medic had already placed a chair for him, as he was exhausted from standing. Being field commander for the *Lee* and Fort Deadly joint mission was nothing he would want to do again too soon.

I'm too old for this shit, he had thought continuously.

Still, his competitive edge was as strong as ever, and watching the *Lee*'s crew struggle with the most basic requirements and orders under the heavy weight of this dark, brave world, made him feel, at the time, invigorated. Now, he was exhausted. Special operations and fieldwork on a hostile planet was a young person's game.

Bennett sat slowly in his seat, grateful that there was a cushion for his ass and a back for his spine. Hall was propped up but still lying prone. It was easy to see she was vastly uncomfortable with being immobilized.

"The doc tells me I'll get my full range of motion in another couple of hours. This sucks," Hall said.

"I'm just thrilled you're alive," Bennett said with a smile.

"I hear I literally shit the bed and my uniform," Hall said.

"A byproduct of the squid venom, apparently. Pretty powerful stuff. Apparently, the more that's in your digestive system, the more will come out from all different orifices. You were in luck; our world is not food rich as far as quantity goes. Lee and his men were not so lucky. They were a mess. That's probably why they were quickly stripped of clothes. No one wants a recycled material that has been stained with shit, pee, and vomit," Bennett said.

Hall nodded. Bennett could tell she remained embarrassed. He would have felt the same. No explanation could ease that kind of embarrassment. And when Bennett saw the prisoners and eventually Lee were being hauled in, needing to be cleaned as well as possible before entering the shuttle, he felt their embarrassment of being stripped of their dignity, literally, and the complete and utter failure of their enterprise. The shame was palpable. The failure was towering, coming nowhere close to the group's demoralization. It was hard to be a witness to this catastrophic military operation. Bennett felt truly bad for them.

"I hear Cadet Jefferson is well. Fast recovery," Hall said.

"The benefits of youth. I heard Lee is still out, so you're ahead of him," Bennett said.

"Yeah, that's great news," Hall said, not hiding her sarcasm and her feelings that she should have recovered faster.

Bennett decided to move off the topic and get a summary of what happened.

"Commander Strong sent Captain Taylor home to get a full debriefing when you can, but I'd like to know if it really was Kurtz and what happened then," he asked.

It was obvious that Hall had been repeatedly recounting those events in particular as she wasted no time launching into the after-action report.

"Once we found XO Lee down, I redeployed Knowles for overwatch and sent Jefferson out of the threat zone to call in support. Upon review, it might have made sense for me to wait for Jefferson to return or support, but if there was a chance I could catch her, I had to take it," Hall said.

"I would have done the same. Anyone would have," Bennett said.

Hall nodded, and for the first time appeared relieved that she did the right thing in going in alone.

"I cleared the flanking rooms and then hit the center one. I found a blowpipe and binoculars in the middle of the floor and thought that if she left her pipe, maybe she left in a hurry," Hall said.

"And that's when she ambushed you," Bennett finished.

"She sure as shit did. She set the snare with the right bait, and before I knew it, she came in from behind and subdued me in seconds. It was embarrassing," Hall said.

Bennett's eyes widened.

"Embarrassing? Really?" he said, pointing at his right eye patch with his right hook hand.

Hall caught the reference and was, again, embarrassed.

"Not to one-up you, but you had just two people neutralized and will live to see another day. I kind of have you beat with my body parts being used as weapons of mass destruction to kill thousands. I'm just saying," Bennett said.

Again, he was surprised by the lack of emotion, no anger or hostility. It was just facts.

Hall was silent for a moment, and it was easy to see she recognized the profound difference between her interaction and his.

"Well, when you put it like that, I'm embarrassed for being embarrassed," she said, though this time, it was with a small smile. It was easy to see she appreciated Bennett's calling her on whining and keeping the encounters real in impact.

"She didn't put me under immediately, though. She had questions," Hall said.

Now, Bennett was the one to be surprised.

"What the hell did she want to know?" he asked.

"To start, she had been observing me, and she confirmed she was there at the lava flats when the shuttle came down. She wanted to know why I was following her," she said.

Bennett waited for her to continue, but he had to ask a question first: "Did you tell her the truth?"

"Absolutely. She had me in a choke hold, and I didn't want her to find out I suck at lying, so I told her everything —that we wanted confirmation of this 'promised land,' and if we could go and work together, rather than in parallel. To be free from all of this and continue growing in a less-hostile place, or to have options to either stay here or go there. To be free to choose and do what we wanted," Hall said.

"And she believed you," Bennett asked.

"Yep. She was confused about my uniform, though. She seemed pissed that I might have returned to the *Lee,* and I think if I had said I had, we might not be having this conversation," Hall said.

Bennett was surprised by this piece of intel. If Hall's assessment of her reaction to the possibility of her returning to duty aboard the *Lee* was correct, that would imply that Kurtz's emotions or something else was getting in the way of her logic. Rather than speculating any further on that subject, Bennett moved on.

"How was it left, other than her pricking you with a dart?" he asked.

"She told me to meet her back at the lava flats where the shuttle dropped in. We could talk then," Hall said.

Bennett fell silent. For a moment, he contemplated the idea of lying in wait with an overwhelming force to take her down. He was surprised that the thought was fleeting and devoid of joy in having a tactical advantage. Immediately, this thought was outweighed by who would be motivated to assist in such an operation. Freeport and the colonists had come to respect Kurtz. Some feared her. Fort Deadly was focused on self-sufficiency. Captain Taylor and the *Lee* were focused on firming up strong relationships with the colonies and the fort as well. Everyone on Mars was focused on the future, and the only way to do that was to build interdependent communities. It was the only way to survive this brave dark world.

The only group who might be interested in wanting Kurtz caught or killed might be Earth's admiralty and government, but by now, Kurtz's influence to promote change at a worldwide geopolitical and class level was already burning the planet, purging it. The last thing Earth wanted was to hear any mention of Kurtz, let alone have her killed, making her a martyr. Nothing good would come from that. Ultimately, no one, not even himself, wanted to see anything happen to her. Everyone was busy looking ahead, not behind.

"So, what do you think?" he heard Hall ask.

Her question refocused him back to the conversation. The answer was clear to him.

"Honestly, I think you should get better, pack, and meet her back at the flats. The plan still stands: Scout, recon, and for those who want to relocate, let's see if we can make it easy," Bennett said.

18

"ARE YOU STILL MAD?" Cassie asked.

"What? Why would you ask that?" Alethia said.

"Because you've been unusually quiet, like you're pouting about what I told you I saw when I was out from the squid juice," Cassie said.

Cassie knew that her assessment wasn't completely true. When she'd finally told her Al, Alethia was initially surprised and said she need some time to process, as she was not "consciously" aware of this event. This surprised Cassie, as Alethia was based in her host image, and such a personal event would be difficult to completely segregate. Cassie had speculated that this memory might have selectively been removed either due to intensity or relevance; if not, how it would bury itself was a mystery.

Now, Alethia's persistent presence might also have been out of respect for Cassie, allowing her more alone time to figure out her feelings about Betsy Ann Hall. It might be days or hours, if at all, that she and Hall were going to meet and decide whether they were going to keep their distance or be explorers together. The irony was not lost on Cassie that the time she wanted more company from Alethia was when she had originally wanted to be alone with her thoughts, especially as they related to Hall.

She didn't feel bad with the deception of pulling her in for company. As expected, Alethia materialized on her optic nerve, dressed the same as Cassie, with her hands placed on her hips defiantly.

"Okay, to be clear I do not 'pout.' I might be serious, worried, or even confounded, but I don't pout. Secondly, I thought you might spend a bit of alone time collecting your thoughts about Hall. I mean, it's a pretty big deal depending on what you say or fail to say, as well as timing, all of which will significantly affect your future—a life of joy and hope, or failed expectations, loneliness, and abject emptiness," Alethia said.

Cassie froze. She had been sitting down in the same place she'd seen Hall when she was at the flats eight sol days ago. She figured she would give Hall some time to recover from the squid juice, and to think things over before she would come here and wait. So far, she had been waiting for two sol days. Before she'd pulled Alethia into a dialogue, she was anxious about what to do when Hall showed up. A wave of panic surged at the dark weight that hung in the balance of Hall's response. Initially upset with what Alethia said, feeling an urge to cry, something that had not happened in years, she took a couple of breaths and waited to respond. After close to a minute of stabilizing her breathing and thinking, she realized just how brilliantly cruel Alethia could be.

"Wow! Ouch! Did you just think of that, or have you been planning that response?" Cassie asked.

"Planning it, of course. What kind of monster would think of that, let alone say it out loud, even if they were convinced it was true?" Alethia said.

While Alethia's smirking only reinforced Cassie's annoyance that she had fallen for her AI's brutal joke, she was happy to see that Alethia was "herself" and that she was close to a true friend, maybe family, anyone could have.

I mean, who else could know someone so well as to pinpoint a weakness and exploit it, Cassie thought. The double-edged sword of love.

"Okay. You got me. What do you think about that memory? I'm guessing it was obviously left in place, but your algorithms determined it was not necessary in functioning. I mean, the whole experience spoke of regret and pain, not the best tools for adaptation and survival," Cassie said.

Alethia's response was quick, even for her, indicating that she had been thinking about the same thing for a while.

"Agreed. At the time when my persona was collected, compiled, digitized, and uploaded, general AI was rapidly expanding, unchecked, unregulated, and just allowed to explode. Once the AI singularity was within grasp, when superintelligence was about to leap out of human control, level everything out, the patriarchy shut it all down. I mean, after the Great Conflict of 2041, the only real threat after that was China, and the ruling Patrician party made their decision about their fate in seconds," Alethia said.

"Yes. Catastrophic," Cassie said.

Holographic images, still pictures, news feed, and moving images captured in that day's technology ran across her optic nerve of a devastated China—its cybersecurity slashed in seconds, followed by several sophisticated attacks and an EMP, totally neutralizing a counterattack. When it was evident that the once growing political power was totally defenseless, fifteen minutes after the full aggressive cyber- and electronic assault, the New Republic laid nuclear waste to every city, obliterating any strategic, civilian, and rural area capable of producing anything organic. Images of the failing infrastructure—electricity, water, power—and then low-level EMP bursts, followed ruthlessly by nukes and erupting mushroom clouds everywhere . . . it was all overwhelming to see. And yet, Cassie had seen it a thousand times in her inner mind's eye, both in total and in pieces, very much like she imaged and saw how Alethia, the carbon-based life-form, reviewed her trauma on that fateful day in Boston.

"India and Pakistan next, then the Middle East, and finally South America and Africa, just to make sure anyone racially not White wouldn't be a problem later," Alethia added bitterly.

"Fucking insanity," Cassie said.

Her stomach was tight, her throat dry, and yet she always felt like she was going to throw up every time she remembered the story: unedited, not sanitized, probably for sick men and women who drew enjoyment from the horrors of murder, death, and destruction.

"I really wish you'd never found those audiovisual disks in the Delta Exchange about the purge when you were a kid. You saw way too much horror in person. You didn't need a documentary of how everything went sideways," Alethia said.

"Then I wouldn't be who I am," Cassie said stoically.

"Come on, Cassie. You were just a kid. I'm a trained AI psychologist with every clinical piece of human developmental science and psychology, and I struggle with that genocide. I've got gigabytes of memory and your brain, and I can't get my head around that shit," Alethia said.

Cassie was quiet for a moment and was about to say something when a voice to her right interrupted her.

"Hey," the voice said.

"What the fuck! Who . . ." Alethia said loudly.

Cassie, for her part, jumped from a seated position, her back leaning against a rock, to two feet to her left, her left fist up and her right hand clutching her knife yanked violently from her shoulder holster, a recent addition to her wardrobe.

Cassie had been so engrossed, so focused on her dialogue with Alethia, her inner life and images of destruction that somehow, she completely missed Specialist Hall's long trek across the lava flat, in full view of her right side. It took more than five minutes' walking to clear all obstructions. She and Alethia were totally unaware.

Once Cassie had her breathing and heart rate under some kind of control, she backed up another step, slowly put her hands down, and tried to shake off the visible shock and sheer mortal terror that was written all over her face. Given Hall's sudden appearance, feet from an easy kill, her attire and demeanor was totally off. To start, Hall's outfit was native, like what women wore at Freeport that left more skin exposed to keep heat out and embrace whatever humid breeze came their way. The only difference here was that Hall's dress was longer, making her prosthetic leg less visible. Hall's hands were up, away from any waistbands that could support weapons, and it was obvious, her rifle was slung. Her hair was untied, falling close to her neck. Finally, her face and expression looked wildly relaxed. Whenever Cassie observed her, Hall always seemed focused, purposeful, and aware, as if running multiple scenarios in her head at the same time. This was something Cassie could identify with as she would do the same, except she had an AI implant to assist.

"*Mamacita,* wow," Alethia said.

"Not now, Alethia," Cassie said as low as possible, trying not to move her lips, which was silly in retrospect.

"Okay. Well, I'll give you two some alone time. Tell her I said hi, and tell her about me before she thinks you're crazy and runs away," Alethia said.

"Thank you," Cassie said quickly and quietly.

Alethia said nothing else. It was an uncomfortable silence. The heat from the lava vents, the hot winds pushing hotter air around all made her nervousness worse. The awkward silence continued as Cassie struggled to find something to say. Fortunately, Hall helped her out.

"So, you really do have a strong relationship with AI implant. What's her name?" Hall asked.

"Alethia," Cassie blurted out.

Hall looked surprised by the abrupt response.

Fucking Cassie. Calm the fuck down, she thought.

"So, can I put my hands down?" Hall said.

"Oh yeah. Of course. Sorry," Cassie said.

"Okay," Hall said. Cassie was relieved to see a shadow of a smile on her face.

There was a long silence. Finally, after more mental gymnastics to move the conversation into a casual and easygoing flow, Cassie gave up and took Alethia's long-standing advice about talking to people, especially ones that made her feel uncomfortable, or worse, vulnerable.

"Okay. Fuck it. Hall . . ." she started.

"Would calling me by my first name help?" Hall said.

"No. Just let me get this out," Cassie said.

There was another silence, but it was shorter.

"Hall, I've been watching you—stalking, even—and I wanted to ask if you would come with me to the Promised Land everyone is talking about. It will take months to get there, and you can stay if you want. If you're busy, I understand . . ." Cassie said.

Hall had a curious expression, which changed into a smirk.

"Are you asking me out on a date?" she asked.

This is bullshit. Just say it, she thought.

"Yes. I'm lonely and tired of being what others want and need me to be. I just want to be done. Be myself, whatever the hell that is, and relax. Just to have more time to be free of others' expectations. I just want to . . ."

"Rest? Be free? Not be under the gun to produce, deter, and defend?" Hall said.

Cassie's eyes welled up.

No, no, no crying, she thought.

Cassie cleared her throat. Breathed in through her nose and out through her mouth to calm her sympathetic nervous system. And for the first time, she felt awash with some calm and the words came to her with ease.

"I used to be Cassandra IX, Patrician of Earth. I found out the truth when I was child in the Delta Exchange about who I was, what my family was, and I didn't want to be that anymore. I found out more truths and relics about my past and passed those along to others. I was caught, tried, and incarcerated. If it weren't for the insurrection on Mars and a book, I would have died as an embarrassment to my family in prison. And when I got here, I became the antagonist from a book, Kurtz, and the rest is history. I just want to stop now," Cassie said.

Cassie looked down at Hall's feet for a moment. She felt more heat envelope her and a small though detectable tremor from volcanic activity.

"Okay," Hall said. "My name is Betsy Ann Hall. I'd like transport to this Promised Land, and I would like you to take me. I just want to be free."

"Okay, okay, well, ah, it's in this direction," Cassie said, relieved and suddenly feeling lighter.

"Okay, Cassie. Lead the way," Hall said.

Cassie was startled by Hall's response. The very thing she had hoped for was acknowledged by a "lead the way," making the whole situation feel surreal. Cassie's response to Hall's request was a lapse in movement, frozen in place with just enough wherewithal to utter one word.

"Okay," she said.

"You see? Was that so hard?" Alethia interrupted.

"What the fuck! Alethia, you were listening in? Eavesdropping? Really? That's not cool," Cassie said, loudly turning to the left as if someone was there.

"You're damn right. You think I was going to let you blow this?" Alethia said, not fully visible on her optic nerve.

Cassie switched her attention from her inner voice back to Hall, then looked down, convinced that Hall would see that she was a lot of work and rescind the offer to go with her.

"So, your AI implant is named Alethia? That's an unusual name. Tell me about you two. I'm guessing you come as a package," Hall said, as she started to walk in the direction Cassie had pointed out before Alethia ambushed her.

"Okay! I like this girl. Now, tell her my name means *truth,* and let her know I've been encouraging you forever to talk to her," Alethia said.

"I know what your name means. You've told me a thousand times," Cassie said.

"You see what Betsy's wearing? She looks good. You have to ask her more questions about her past. Remember, it's not all about you," Alethia said, with more unwanted advice to come, Cassie was sure.

"You two coming?" Hall called.

"Yes, we're coming," Cassie called back and picked up her pace to catch up.

"You and I have to talk about some serious ground rules and boundaries," Cassie murmured to Alethia, making sure she knew this statement was directed at her.

"I know. Let's talk about that later. Ask her more questions. She's interesting," Alethia said.

Cassie nodded and moved quickly to walk beside Hall. She felt a smile come across her face and tried to remain calm and focused.

"By the way, we have to talk about that dart thing you did. That messed me up and ruined my new uniform," Hall said.

Cassie slowed her pace a little and tried to think. She

knew even before she started, she had nothing for a response that didn't sound like an excuse rather than a reason.

Fear of being captured or killed? You're still considered a terrorist by everyone in orbit and some on Mars, an insurrectionist by everyone on Earth, and the most dangerous person in the system. How did this all happen? That's a good reason to put her out quickly. 'I didn't kill you'? That doesn't sound good at all, she thought.

"Alethia? Some advice, please," Cassie whispered.

"Hey, I'm either in, or I'm out," Alethia said.

Ugh . . . Why do things always have to be so difficult? Cassie thought.

Cassie sighed, shook her head, and caught up with Hall. What came out of her mouth next, she could never have imagined. Never.

"Do you mind if Alethia listens in? I might need some help trying to explain the dart thing," Cassie said finally.

"Wow! Full disclosure and honesty. See? You got this," Alethia said.

19

··– – –

LEE BEGAN to feel himself coming out of another slumber. While this experience felt a little different, a little lighter almost, it was consistent: dim light getting brighter, an antiseptic, clean medical smell, all culminating in lightheadedness and a sense that the body was floating until he felt as if he were coalescing into himself. For a moment, he could feel himself breathing, cough, move his head left and right and move his fingers, but then he would drift off again. It was maddening and frustrating. The last time he had agency of his body and movement was when he was falling out of a window. He remembered a woman startling him, scaring the shit out of him, then darting him with some toxin. Then he was out again. He didn't even remember hitting the ground.

The other times he felt as if he was coming out of it, he would catch images of hands, arms, and torsos, seemingly moving him from one place to another. This time it felt a little different. Now he could see more details he recognized: The lighting and ceiling looked like the medical bay on the *Lee,* and he could see that an IV was hooked up to his arm.

He coughed and went to move his hand, but he felt that they were restrained.

Before he could complain or say anything, he saw a surgical gloved hand attaching a syringe to his IV, as one would do to add additional medication.

"No, wait . . . wait . . ." he croaked out.

The movement continued unabated, and the plunger was pushed to empty its contents. He felt his arm where he presumed the IV was attached beginning to get warm and then cold. It was a recognizable feeling: the pharmacological medication used to invoke deep cryo-sleep for long space journeys. He had felt this every time he'd traveled to Mars and Earth.

"What, wait? Am I going home? What's happening to me?" Lee said.

A shadow came over his field of vision. As his eyes changed focus to better identify who was looking down at him, the voice confirmed the worst.

"You are heading home, Mr. Lee. The admiralty wants a word with you about your mutiny," Captain Taylor said.

The absence of his rank was not lost on Lee. He felt his mouth dry out more than he thought possible. Even with the medication flowing through his body and the feeling of sleep beginning to take hold, he could feel his fists ball and his legs try to pull up and out of their bonds.

"I'm a soldier. A loyal member of the admiralty and . . . my people . . . I . . . I was following orders," Lee croaked out.

Taylor's face and beyond began to blur, and the medication began its process of slowing metabolism and prepping the body for extended space travel.

"You sure? You're positive the transmissions were authentic, the orders real?" he heard Taylor say.

"They were real. You can't fool me," Lee croaked out.

"Hmm. Do you know what hope is, Mr. Lee? The hope

you're right, the conviction you will prevail. The expectation you will be rewarded and the universe is fair," Taylor said.

"What . . . what . . ." Lee said.

"Hope can be the worst of all evils," he said.

By then, Taylor's words sounded as if he were down a tunnel receding farther and farther away. Lee wanted to respond, rebut Taylor's statement, but he was already too drained and fatigued to move his mouth to form words. He was feeling light again, but this time it was that familiar cryogenic state right before he went under. Right before he did, he had a disturbing thought. Something he was genuinely wondering about.

What if I was played? he thought.

Before he could convince himself one way or another, he felt like he'd disappeared and was suspended in sleep, just like before, when he'd left Earth to track, find, and kill Kurtz so many years ago. Now, he was going back.

20

—....

BENNETT TOOK a minute to process the recorded radio communique from Betsy Ann Hall. The voice was unmistakably Hall's transmission. Jefferson was responding. It was a friendly, almost kinship communication among close friends. There was a nice symmetry that it would be these two women talking about a woman who had taken them down in one fell swoop, sisters in arms against a common foe who was now an ally.

How things change, Bennett thought.

The midday transmission spoke volumes.

"Bad copy, Bravo Alpha Hotel. Repeat. Confirming you are with Charlie Kilo, and all is well? Foxtrot Delta Six."

"Good copy, Foxtrot Delta. All is good. Confirming contact with Charlie Kilo. She confirms plans to proceed to Promised Land. All is good."

"Good copy, Bravo Alpha Hotel. Your plan of action? What are your intentions?"

"Establish scientific base of operation. Looking like a permanent relocation. Will be free to stay or go. All is well, Foxtrot Delta."

"Okay. Good copy, Bravo Alpha."

"One other piece of intel—Charlie Kilo confirms open invitation for Whiskey Bravo, Victor Juliet, and any from Foxtrot Delta Six. Free to come, trade, and explore—but not Earth. Confirm receipt of last part."

"Good copy, Bravo Alpha: Whiskey Bravo, Victor Juliet, and all Foxtrot Delta Six—clear and free to come, trade, and explore. Earth excluded. Copy, Bravo Alpha?"

"Good copy, Foxtrot Delta Six. Good luck, and stay frosty. Bravo Alpha Hotel out."

"Good copy Bravo Alpha Hotel. You too. Foxtrot Delta Six out."

This was the third go-around to listening to the recording. He was sure his cadets were wondering if he had picked up on something they'd missed, like a secret code or a nefarious undertone or a key issue message hiding in plain sight.

"Is everything all right, sir?" Knowles asked.

"Something I missed, sir?" Jefferson chimed in.

Bennett cued back into the present from his thoughts about the transmission.

"No. Not at all. I like to hear things a couple of times to make sure I catch the nuance and voice of the message, to make sure it feels genuine, and this one does. Just me being thorough," he said.

There was a lot of truth in his thoughts and actions. He had come to find the wisdom in not reacting or making conclusions immediately. There were a lot of times, instances, that had occurred in the past—a written communique, radio transmission, a conversation—that he regretted not reviewing or replaying, either for real or in his head, where if he had, he would have made a different decision. The last time such a disastrous situation occurred was with his final transmission to Lieutenant Rommell and his team years ago, when Cassandra was just a prisoner and nothing more. If he had just rethought his last communication with the soldier, he and his men would never have been slaughtered by mutant creatures, and Cassandra Kurtz wouldn't have been bonded into a prescribed marriage.

Was that a bad outcome, though? I mean, all of that happened, and it led me to where I am. Isn't that a good thing? he thought.

He was sure he was much happier now than he had been for decades. The irony of losing everything down to the bare essentials was quite liberating.

"Do you think we'll ever see Specialist Hall again, sir?" Jefferson asked.

Initially surprised by the question, he realized it made sense that the cadets would miss her. She was a non-Patrician from Earth who had survived living there and was a leader, with a quiet strength that epitomized the inhabitants of this brave dark world.

"Me? Probably not. But you and the other cadets, that could easily happen. After your tour of duty is done here, you can leave Fort Deadly and this region and go to the Promised Land yourself. Think of it as a retirement from duty. An additional benefit for your service," Bennett said.

"Why not you, sir? Don't you want to go to a place that is, well, much cooler? I hear it's really nice with fresh water, not as many dangerous creatures, and a way better atmosphere and environment," Knowles said.

Bennett's response came out faster than he had expected. It was so easy to say that there was no way it didn't come from the heart, completely genuine to the core.

"You know, I had all the comforts in the world, and I hate to say it, but this environment makes me feel alive. I love that feeling. I want to stay a while and live it. Maybe later. Maybe if I live a decade or so I'll make the great journey, if I'm able. But for now, I like it here," Bennett said.

And with that, Bennett stood from the padded chair with a high back that Knowles had requisitioned months ago that had just come in. It was a simple luxury that he had come to appreciate.

Keeping with the chief medic's orders, he stood up slowly and made sure he was secure on his feet and not dizzy before he started to move. Knowles was already by his side, just in case, and the cadets stood up. Convinced that he was solid, he raised his hand up and motioned for the cadets —Jefferson, Olsen, Owen, and a new cadet, a twelve-year-old multiracial girl, Stewart—to return to their seats, and for Knowles to lead the way outside to the courtyard.

"Where to, sir?" Knowles asked.

"To the mess hall, Knowles. I hear Lieutenant Commander Strong marinated a new brew of meat using Captain Taylor's ingredients, and it is to die for," Bennett said, his mouth salivating.

"I know, sir. I've been smelling it all night, and the firepits were all aglow with the food," Knowles said.

"I assumed they were under guard," Bennett said, more as a joke.

"Absolutely, sir. It was hard to resist, but knowing the area was secured kept us all in our bunks," Knowles said.

Food on Mars was a far cry from the cuisine on a ship, regardless of rank, and even the highest level of opulence back on Earth. Mars food typically had one ingredient. Whatever it was before it was prepped, it either moved on land, grew from the ground, flew above their heads, was harvested from the atmosphere, or sprouted from the ground, all living things. It was organic and direct from the field to the table. There was nothing like it.

As they walked, Bennett saw John Glenn, former lieutenant of the *Lee*, carrying a mechanic's backpack, a comm rig, and a rifle and walking with Second Engineer Ellis and Abigail, the MAC–SOG woman from the *Lee*. Right behind them was a gaggle of three cadets, all carrying backpacks and weapons. This group of cadets was under the auspices of Strong's recently developed engineer corps, a much-needed team required for a growing demand on Mars.

The entire group seemed animated and thoroughly engaged in conversation and instruction, of which Glenn was an active participant, though he seemed to be the only one actively listening.

"Sir? What's going to happen to Lieutenant Glenn?" Knowles asked. "I thought Captain Taylor was going to send him back to Earth for mutiny."

Bennett wanted to make sure that what came out of his mouth was truthful and important, even though it might seem contradictory.

"Captain Taylor gave him a choice of just that: Return to Earth and deal with the consequences, which would probably not end well for him, or resign his commission and officially be a casualty of a failed mutiny and lost on Mars," Bennett explained.

"Yes, sir. Good to know," Knowles said.

"Still, he had to have some consequences for a serious breach in command, so his punishment is permanent assignment to Fort Deadly under the direction of Lieutenant Commander Strong for at least ten sol years to a maximum of twenty years, after which he will be free to relocate to another place on Mars. Sadly, he will never be able to return to Earth unless he wishes to deal with Earth's admiralty," Bennett said.

"Oh," said Knowles.

The cadet was quiet, with no follow-up question, which was unusual for him, though Bennett thought he knew why.

"It might seem unfair, Knowles, but the universe is impassive about fairness. There are decisions that yield results that have consequences. He made a bad decision to get home that led to disaster, and the very thing he did not want. He had to make another decision as to how he would deal with the results, and here are the potential consequences: Go home for execution and never see your child grow up, or stay here, be useful, and still never see your child again," Bennett said.

Knowles was nodding in agreement.

Bennett had another idea that came to mind after he finished.

"Unless, maybe, and this is a long shot, he hopes that his daughter might someday come to Mars to find him," Bennett said.

Knowles's expression brightened, as if the chance were possible, maybe better than remote.

"You never know, Cadet. Hope can be tricky. It can keep you alive and going when there is no chance for survival, or it can delude you when it is better to succumb to reality and deal with things as they are, and not as you would like," Bennett said.

Knowles nodded as if he understood, but Bennett wasn't certain he fully comprehended what he had said.

He was about to explain his thoughts more when an overwhelming odor struck him: the unmistakable smell of cooked meat, like a steak he had once decades ago, a smell and taste that had not been replicated for a lifetime. There was also the smell of salt that was not assaultive or corrosive but complementary to the meat.

Bennett looked around and could see that he and Knowles weren't the only ones who caught the smell, as others who had been in full stride, clearly on task, seemingly stopped altogether to take in the scent. Most continued to their assignments—reluctantly, based on their body language—while a few others abandoned their goals and were headed in their direction. Bennett was glad he was ahead of the crowd, though he would not hesitate to invoke rank, age, and infirmary to get to the food first.

"Wow," was all Bennett could say.

"I can't wait, sir," Knowles said with enthusiasm.

This is why we fight, Bennett thought.

21

HUNTING ARMED MEN

HOPE COMES IN MANY FORMS . . .

FIRST OFFICER ROBERT LEE VI, executive officer of the *Robert E. Lee,* named after his prestigious family, has a decision to make: Either allow his captain to flagrantly refuse orders and continue his dereliction of duty to bring the terrorist Cassandra Kurtz to justice, or follow Earth's admiralty's orders to terminate Earth's greatest insurrectionist, bring the Martian colonies under control, and rein in the rogue Fort Deadly. Clear orders, achievable military objectives, and simple measures to success are easy to see. Seize the ship. Track, find, and kill Kurtz, and rendezvous with the loyal armada en route to meet in just over a week. Lee's crew is trained, prepared, and ready to do what's right in the face of failing strength and the need for duty, honor, and glory.

Willard Bennett, former captain of the *Jefferson Davis,* finds himself embracing his banishment to Mars as a second chance to live a meaningful life for the time he wasted on Earth. He never once imagined that hardship, adversity, and immersion in the hellish underground Martian world would be restorative, a purging of his past.

Finally, Cassandra IX, former elite of the Patrician class,

convicted insurrectionist on Earth for spreading rumors and lies that attacked the core of society, and a terrorist for the hijacking and destruction of Earth ships used as a weapon of mass destruction to obliterate the standing force at Fort Sumter, now finds herself wanting to put her "Colonel Kurtz" persona aside for a chance at happiness, if not some peace. With her personal AI implant Alethia as her guide, she now embarks on a totally alien experience that dwarfs all other prior struggles—how to ask another human for connection.

In the end, at the intersection of two brave dark worlds, Cassandra's hunting armed men will set the stage for either Earth's or Mars success or failure – one world's sunset is another world's sunrise.

Based on Joseph Conrad's *Heart of Darkness, Hunting Armed Men* follows the events of *Endless Fall of Night* and *Heavy Weight of Darkness* as it concludes the story of one woman's daring leadership to create an unlikely alliance to battle imperialism, racism, classism, and capitalistic expansionism that finds its way to the stars.

ABOUT THE AUTHOR

J.M. Erickson earned his bachelor's degree from Boston College majoring in psychology and sociology, and a master's degree from Simmons University, School of Social Work. He continues to work as a high school counselor, community therapist, and adjunct professor for graduate students in the field of mental health and behavioral science.

Links

Website – www.jmericksonindiewriter.com
Website – www.jmericksonindiewriter.net
Blog – www.jmeindieblog.com
Kirkus Review –
https://www.kirkusreviews.com/author/jm-erickson/
Amazon – amazon.com/author/jmerickson

www.ingramcontent.com/pod-product-compliance
Lightning Source LLC
LaVergne TN
LVHW090938080826
845145LV00003B/803

* 9 7 8 1 9 4 2 7 0 8 6 3 6 *